Hostages of the Sphere

GG Rodgers

I'd like to say thank you to my mother, father, and siblings. I don't know the words to describe how much I love you.

Charlie and Alex… Alex and Charlie, you two are my reason for all the good I ever do. Thanks for being my inspiration.

I'd like to say thank you to my mother, father, and siblings. I don't know the words to describe how much I love you.

Charlie and Alex... Alex and Charlie, you two are my reason for all the good I ever do. Thanks for being my inspiration.

Chapter One: The Great King

Battle smoke from cannons, firearms, and grenades slithered through the air. Two soldiers, dressed in protective armor, wrestled with what appeared to be an oversized lizard and struggled to bring her body to the ground. She stood on her hind legs and was a foot taller than the men. Severe wounds prohibited her from using her full strength. She hissed once a taser clung to her back and sent debilitating shock waves throughout her body.

"Finally!" Said the soldier holding the taser gun as the creature collapsed onto the ground, face first. He nervously looked around.

"Damn it, man! How am I supposed to enjoy it if my pecker's getting electrocuted the whole time?" his partner complained while removing the lower half of his uniform.

"Just be quick about it! I want a turn!"

"Hey!" yelled a third soldier. He approached them with heavy footsteps and an expression of disbelief. "What are you maggots doing over here?!"

"Nothing, sir! W-w-we were bringing it to the lab, sir!" blurted the standing soldier as his partner scrambled from atop the creature.

She was no longer breathing.

"This is *not* what we do! Get her onto the wagon before more of them arrive from the caves. Go! Go!"

The king lifted his head from the mud and gaped while gasping for air. He was still alive. This was the worst attack yet. He could taste gritty clumps of rock particles floating around in his mouth and suffered with each blink as tiny pieces of sand cut the undersides of his eyelids. Everything appeared blurry. He heard moans of agony around him, but his distorted vision left him momentarily disabled. Thick smoke slowly dispersed through the air until the damages could finally be seen. A deafening explosion had left the king's ears ringing and sent the body parts of countless warriors scattered across the ground. A detached tail wiggled and twitched next to him. He wondered to whom it belonged. After realizing that he was no longer a target, he spat into his hands and wiped his eyes. His vision became clearer as he saw men, dressed in protective armor, just like the astronaut spacesuits that he'd seen on television when he was a boy. They wore helmets with large reflecting-glass fronts that made it impossible to see their faces. The men hauled unconscious aboriginal warriors, called Surges, and hoisted them onto the backs of their jeeps. The king couldn't tell whether they were dead or not. Fear, wrapped in anger and guilt, erupted from his belly as he helplessly watched the convoy leave.

Once the jeep engines couldn't be heard anymore, the king pushed his body from the thick mud and rose to his feet. He wailed and cursed under his breath as a sharp pain shot through his right leg. The unfamiliar pressure caused him to fall back into the mud. His leg had been severely broken. His jagged shin bone protruded through his bloody flesh while the rest of his leg dangled involuntarily.

"King Grate! Let us help you!" Two colossal Surges raced to the king. Upon seeing his mangled leg, one of them scooped him up as if he were a small child while the other grabbed his leather satchel and weapons from nearby. The king's battle axe and flail were stained with human blood. He'd killed three; maybe more men this time.

"Return to the caves," ordered the king in the Surges' native tongue. "Find Argan. Argan…," he grunted. His lips were dry and cracked. His head felt as though it weighed fifty moons. His surroundings began to spin; faster and faster, until he fainted in the arms of his faithful soldier.

Deep within the Onyx Caves, lived the last of the Surges and their fearless king. Surges could best be described as salamander-like humans or human-like salamanders. Big ones. The males grew to be seven, sometimes eight feet tall and had strong, broad shoulders. The females were smaller in frame and stood at six or seven feet tall. Their tails were shorter than the males', too. Four fingers and toes on each hand and foot was the norm. Their smooth, scale-free skin had unique patterns and colors that signified their stages of life. Adolescent Surges were speckled with white spots, young adults had brightly colored patterns across their skin, and seniors were darker and monochrome. Besides their inconceivable strength, Surges possessed various powers and abilities such as psychokinesis, superspeed or momentary mind control. Despite what one might assume, the Surges weren't unattractive creatures. They walked upright, had muscular, slender bodies, and had faces quite similar to contemporary humans.

Caves on this planet were as beautiful as they were mysterious. Not only were they home to unique aquatic animals, the caves also led to underground pools that were filled with glimmering lights and allowed passage into deeper layers of the planet. The sweet-smelling water moved to and fro as it pleased. Lit torches, which were placed along the walls, provided golden light that flirted with the water and bounced back up to prance across the stone walls.

The king's chamber was a vast cave that had a section reserved for his weaponry and another for meetings with Surge dignitaries. His bed sat on a higher level of stone and overlooked the space. King Grate now lied in bed, with his injured leg propped on a cushion. Just then, a splash caught his attention. It was a Living Pool puddle that spent most of its time in the king's bedroom. It expanded from the floor until it reached Grate's side and darkened from light green to deep blue.

"I'll be alright. I appreciate your concern," he told it; still speaking the language of the Surges. He released a sigh of relief upon seeing an elder Surge appear at the entrance of the chamber.

"Your Majesty, I have brought the strongwater. May I enter?" she asked. A clay jar rested in her large, gray hands.

The king nodded once then closed his eyes. The Surge hastily approached him and focused on his wounds. His leg was an obvious mark. She also sensed internal bleeding and possibly an aneurysm near his brain. There were at least two cracked ribs. She removed the jar's lid and tilted the container to release a light pink liquid onto his mutilated leg. The substance fizzled and foamed upon touching his skin. King Grate clenched his teeth and winced in pain. His toes curled. His thighs began to spasm. His belly jumped. And his hands balled into tight fists as tears gathered in his eyes. The resuscitation of dimmed cells was excruciating.

He was an alluring man. Standing nearly seven feet tall, he commanded the attention of anyone near without saying a word. His radiant, copper skin was evenly sun kissed. His eyes maintained a youthful glow yet possessed the wisdom of a hundred years. Mother wit and a disarming smile were his aide with friend as well as foe. He was blessed with charm, beauty, and strength beyond measure. Over the years, he'd broken nearly every bone in his body at least once. If it had not been for the pink healing strongwater, he would surely have died from pain or infection years ago.

Tears streamed down Grate's face.

"Relax, my Lord," offered the elder as she continued to pour the pink water over each of his wounds. She watched his shin bone fuse together and the torn flesh mend. All that remained were a few bruises, which would fade within a few weeks. Lastly, she brought the jar to his lips and encouraged him to drink from it.

The sour coolness traveled down his throat in search of all abnormalities. He gulped and thought of her smile. The sun was particularly bright that day. And warm. The bleeding near his liver ceased. Was it the sun or her smile? Her curly, red hair refused to behave no matter how many times she led it behind her ears. The clot in his brain dissolved.

"King Grate," uttered a fatigued Surge, who waited at the entrance of the chamber. She was covered in dirt and blood from battle.

"Argan!" He jumped up from the bed and limped to her. "Thank the stars you're alright!" He wrapped his long arms around her and held her closely. "Any word on the others?"

"My brother is gone. Trepor has been captured." Argan shuddered; unable to cry. Her doleful eyes begged him to tell her that the words were untrue.

The king's knees went weak. He turned to the elder, who still stood beside his bed, and asked for privacy. The puddle migrated underneath the bed.

"Argan, I am so very, very sorry. Trepor was a mighty warrior and incomparable leader. The best friend anyone could have. More than a friend. He was my big brother." He rested his forehead on Argan's and closed his eyes. "I will avenge his death; do you hear me? I promise you. I promise." A searing bolt of anger shot down his chest and landed in his stomach. He moved from her and marched to a shelf that sat in an opposite corner of the room then shoved it over. "Damn him!" He wiped his mouth, using the back of his hand. "The Robot will not stop until he has killed us all. One by one. What does he want? What is his purpose?" he asked, facing the wall. "Why won't he leave us—" He stopped.

Argan stood with her back turned to him and hugged herself. She wept quietly. Grate approached her and gently placed his hands around the base of her neck.

"Argan, have you had strongwater?"

She nodded.

"Good. I want you to go rest. I will find a way to stop this."

Argan sniffled and looked up into his hazel eyes. "Thank you," she managed. She was his confidant and most trusted warrior.

Unlike the others, she only stood at about 5 and a half feet tall and had no tail. She appeared more mammal-like than her peers; but, her deformities were never minded.

Once alone, King Grate returned the overturned shelf to its proper position. Next, he knelt on one knee and retrieved the items that had fallen to the floor. Neat locks of hair fell over his face. His beating heart and racing thoughts had no destination and he felt as if he might go mad. He needed order, in every way. The thought of Trepor's contagious smile and delightful sense of humor brought him a moment of peace. They'd just eaten breakfast together earlier that morning. And now, all that Trepor was or could've become, had permanently transitioned into memories and hopes without anyone's permission.

After cleaning his mess, the king walked toward a corner of the chamber that descended several feet; then whistled. Trickling noises were heard as the puddle rushed from beneath the bed to his side. It suddenly began to swell until it filled the corner and formed a small pool. Grate removed his loin cloth and stepped into the milky-green water as it warmed. It reached his collar bone once he sat. Waves of black paint swirled away from his body and merged with the water. He wore this paint any time he left the caves so that he'd look more Surge than human. He sat back and slowly rotated his ankles and pointed his toes. All the physical pain was gone.

"I think I'm ready for a mate, Grate. It's time for love," Trepor had said that morning.

"You?" laughed Grate. "And give up all of the glorious... fruit of the garden?" He took a bite of his blue peach and grinned.

"Absolutely. Love... I mean *real* love... is rare."

"Oh, they love you!" he chuckled. "You have more admirers than I do. Almost."

"Grate, I'm serious."

"But there's so much out there! And we're so young!" Grate shook his head in disappointment.

"You can't always live your life trading a good thing you already have for what you assume is better. That's not winning."

"Speak for yourself."

"I want to build. And invest. I want to wake up next to someone, who I *know* loves me. Not because of my power or lineage. Someone, who finds my light during the darkest hour. Someone, who knows all of my faults yet motivates me to be better. Someone, who will pour strongwater upon my wounds and think the stars of me all the while."

"Nah. You're just hungry, brother. Try this-"

"King Grate!" Argan sprinted into the chamber, breathless. Trepor sprang up from his chair.

"Robot's army is approaching the caves!"

Since the arrival of the earthlings, Surges had been cautious about not being seen; as they were aware of the mark that humans left on things unfamiliar to them. However, over the past two or three years, an army of robot-looking men had been throwing explosives into the caves and forcing Surges to emerge from hiding. Due to their size and incredible strength, it was almost impossible to capture them. They'd fight until they could fight no longer. Any missing Surge would be assumed dead. No ordinary human, or even group of humans would dare confront one. Most of the population didn't believe that Surges were real to begin with. Grate was certain that the corrupt scientist and ruler of the planet, called Dr. Robot was behind these attacks; he just didn't know why.

Grate's lips trembled as he tried to control his heightening emotions. He then slid down into the steamy pool until he was fully submerged and screamed with all of his might.

Chapter Two: Planet Bethiter

By the close of the Old World's 21st century, every "natural" disaster, disease epidemic, stock market fluctuation, political election, passed law, social revolution, technological advancement, information leak, and even fashion trend was the result of the ten most powerful families playing God. For hundreds of years, these families had been trading and buying the rights to parts of the planet - and its inhabitants. They'd play sinister games that gravely impacted the land and people that belonged to their rival families. On the same note, the families would invest in protecting and advancing their own lands. These exchanges of power and shifts in misfortune throughout various populations were intricate parts of a far more callous plan. For in the end, when the Earth was no more, the top families would welcome a select few to travel into space and continue their lives on another planet.

What would've been 2114 on the Old World was year 23 on Bethiter. This new planet was much larger than the former one. It was mainly an enormous, cosmic body of water that casually changed colors. This bright, water-rich atmosphere was occupied by massive aquatic creatures that were nothing like anything seen before on Earth. There were beasts that had many heads and some that appeared as shooting stars slashing through the water. There were others that moved about by devouring themselves whole at first, then reappeared by birthing their own bodies.

A solid mass of land, which was fully submerged in water, rested at the center of Bethiter. In preparation for the arrival of the air breathers, an enormous man-made glass sphere was engineered and placed around the landmass. An exceptionally intelligent filtration system utilized the water from outside of the sphere to produce oxygen within. Here, a lively civilization of humans and animals from the Old World were supplied with a habitable, stormless climate. A synthetic sun orbited the sphere that provided daylight, moonlight, and warmth. With the installation of the outer glass sphere came the extinction of countless species of wildlife and types of vegetation. Interestingly, the sphere, artificial sunlight, and moist atmosphere also birthed new trees and plants, that wouldn't have existed on the planet prior to the humans' arrival.

Bethiter's land surfaces had an abundance of character. There were countless valleys, caves, and mountains that were an eye's treat to behold. Much of the planet's floor was made of various types of corral and shells. Its regions fell under three categories: The Pasturage, The Community, and The Stretch.

The Pasturage is where those, who were affluent on Earth, lived. These were the families that had generational wealth and riches to spare. The Pasturage was an exquisite, suburban area that seemed to have it all. Plush, verdant yards were adorned with unnecessarily large abodes. Large LED light bars continually shone down on the neighborhood to ward off native creatures and evaporate unwanted waters. With the exception of the fact that no one younger than twenty-three years old lived there and no newborns lived beyond a week, it was very much like the Old World. Curvaceous maples, tall pines, enormous magnolias, and other trees and bushes of the sort adorned the yards. Large, gaudy homes with columns and guest houses and three-car garages complemented the plush, manicured lawns. There was a bright, clean supermarket that provided organic (earthly) products, a fancy fitness club that offered yoga, Pilates, cycle class, and more, and a top-of-the-line hospital that hired the best trained staff. Clothing boutiques with the latest fashions and costly beauty salons could also be found there. Just as the rich and powerful were on Earth, these residents were particular about their privacy and safety; and they only welcomed members from The Community within their gates if they were going to be the help. A towering stone wall bordered the posh little district and was constantly manned by armed security guards.

Beyond the walls of the planet's elite was The Community. An uninviting, iron fence that had barbed wire woven throughout it surrounded the settlement. Most of the able-bodied Community members worked for the rich in The Pasturage. Although this is where the "commoners" lived, there was nothing common about them. Because of the fare for the ticket to relocate to Bethiter, it should be understood that these people were also rich... at one point in their lives. These were the movie stars, professional athletes, nationally syndicated talk show hosts, top Wall Street investors, and people of the sort. Their friends and families were also there, if someone had been so kind as to purchase a spacecraft ticket. This neighborhood was more rustic and wet than The Pasturage. The natural characteristics of the planet were apparent and there was no room for doubt about whether they were on the Old World or not. Thick moss coated the grounds and there seemed to always be new puddles appearing, even in the homes.

The vegetation glowed with unique colors and could be compared to those of pre-historic Earth. Mild-mannered animals, which were like earthly insects, rodents, amphibians, and air-breathing fish were a part of everyday life here. And although Community members were considerably poor and dowdy, they were happy. And their children were happy too. There was a common area, in the heart of the community, where people gathered to buy, sell, and trade goods. There was also a place comparable to an urgent care clinic that served its purpose with a host of midwives and doulas for the women. There was a vocational school that taught its students practical skills such as cooking, mechanics, and carpentry. Everyone put forth great effort into remaining positive and being grateful for having made it out of the Old World alive.

Past the mossy planes of The Community rested unchartered territory that was feared and forbidden to be explored. In fact, the top five rules of the new land were: no discussing the Old World, no fraternizing with those of a different class, no flying attempts, no consuming unpasteurized water, and no visiting The Stretch. It was said that The Stretch was where only the foolish or brave dared to go. Sometimes members of both The Pasturage and Community would venture there if they were terminally ill, and tired of living, yet too afraid of dying at their own hands; but, that was rarely discussed and shrugged off as hearsay.

The Stretch hosted wild beasts, mysterious forests, and the blackest caves ever known. The grounds were covered by smooth indentations that had been shaped by water flow and in some places. Over the years, imaginative colonizers created maps and shared fables regarding The Stretch and its creatures. Not only were the unnerving stories entertaining; they also kept people's curiosities satisfied behind their respective walls.

Despite the mandate, there was of course one human; who dared to live in the merciless wilderness apart from civilization. King Grate's brave heart and natural ability to take charge, made him an ideal leader for the Surges after the disappearance of their chief. Their specific whereabouts were unknown to the rest of the population, although it was rumored that they dwelled somewhere between the Forbidden Valleys and Living Forest.

Of course, there was regular water for drinking, bathing, and things of the sort; but, there were two other distinct types of water. Healing strongwater, which was found in the Breathing Valley, reversed any wounds and injuries it touched. Then, there were the Living Pools, which changed their color and form as they pleased and roamed the planet freely. This sentient water had the ability to revive the dead; if it chose to do so. The Pools seemed to dance with themselves as they would well, swell, and leap far and wide;

reaching for the prodigious mass of water that rested on the outside of the sphere. They were smart enough to avoid the new settlers and since no one toured The Stretch, the healing strongwater wasn't procurable to humans either.

Chapter Three: Parlimont Manor

      Out of all the large, elaborate homes within The Pasturage's gates, Parlimont Manor was the largest and most elaborate. The Parlimonts was Bethiter's wealthiest family and awarded many of the luxuries found on the old planet.

      Parlimont Manor was incredibly still and sober that Tuesday night. Though occupied by a butler, a driver, three maids, two bodyguards, a chef, a doorman and, of course, the Parlimonts-nothing could be heard at the estate. The mansion was remarkable. Its lower level hosted a vintage wine cellar, five-lane bowling alley, cutting-edge movie theater, luxury spa and cigar lounge. The main level had elegant double winding staircases in the front foyer that rested beneath an antique crystal chandelier. There was also a wall-to-wall library, professional fitness center, presidential office, grand two-island kitchen, private auditorium and a few other extraordinary chambers that were rarely used. On the third floor were mostly bedrooms and bathrooms. The master suite was in the West wing. The nursery was in the East.

      A hybrid hue of gold and royal blue wallpaper with cream-colored trim decorated the nursery. The handcrafted 12-piece nursery set was also painted a cool cream to match the trim. In a dim corner of the room stood a beautiful dark woman, whose eyes were closed, and lips were moving; as if she were praying. She was the lead maid, turned wet-nurse. Hampton Parlimont, Jr. and his wife, Serenity "Sara" Parlimont, were also there. Hampton was a tall and lanky fellow, who was handsome in his own way. Whatever he lacked in charisma, kindness or charm was compensated for by his last name. Sara was svelte and lovely. She possessed the sort of beauty that remained even on her worst days.

The couple held each other closely as they watched their newborn daughter sleep peacefully in her crib. It seemed that with each breath that the doll-faced infant took, her tearful mother released a heavy sigh of relief. Hampton gently stroked Serenity's back, then moved one of her scarlet curls away from her brow to behind her ear. Moments later, Serenity dropped her head, only to make her hair fall back in front of her face.

"You should lie down. You lost a lot of blood this time. Remember what the doctor said?"

"No. I'm not going anywhere. I've already told you that," Sara stated with conviction.

Hampton glanced back at the maid in the corner then removed a handkerchief from his blazer pocket and blotted the tears that began to stream down Sara's face. Her gaze met his; and there they stood, staring at one another until a melody chimed from Hampton's pocket.

"It's Edgar," he reported before answering the call. "Hello, Hampton speaking…"

"Oh no," Sara whispered. She turned to the maid, who stood behind them. "Margot, what day is it?" she asked with brooding eyes.

"It's Tuesday," answered Margot. She swallowed hard.

Sara wiped her nose and looked toward the ceiling. She thought for a moment; counted to five. "No, that's not right. Five? Or is it six?" she said to herself.

"Please give Claudette our love. And let us know if you need anything," Hampton spoke into the phone. "Alright, now. Goodbye."

"The baby?" Sara asked.

Hampton nodded and returned his phone to his pocket. "The Vanhooven's son just passed away. On his seventh day."

Margot dropped her head.

Sara placed her hand on her aching abdomen and fixed her unblinking gaze on her three-day-old baby.

Just then, a loud voice could be heard booming downstairs in the spacious foyer. The voice rang through Hampton's ears and caused the hairs on the back of his neck to stiffen.

"My word. Could it be?" Hampton uttered. The intensity in his eyes frightened his wife. "Stay here, Sara," he commanded as he rushed toward the nursery's exit.

As he reached the large cream double doors, an urgent knock rattled against them. Margot gasped and stepped away from the wall. Sara's nostrils flared. Hampton quickly opened the door to find their new maid, Lucille, frozen in fear. One of the bodyguards was running towards the staircase. The other, with firearm in hand, stood on guard as he peered down onto the floor below.

"What is it, Lucille? Who's here?" spat a white-faced Parlimont. He stood on the tips of his toes and craned his neck to view his surroundings.

The wide-eyed maid stood before him; unable to speak. Hampton belched, causing tangy vomit to spurt into his mouth. He felt as if he was on the verge of insanity while hoping that the voice he'd heard didn't belong to whom he'd believed. He reached for his handkerchief only to remember that he'd left it with Sara. This frustrated him even more. He swallowed.

"Well?" His bitter breath escaped his lips. "Who is it, girl?!"

Unsure of what he may do to the young maid, Margot sprang forward and rushed towards them. "Lucille, sweetheart… who is it? Tell momma who's here," she whispered.

Lucille nodded to her mother. "It's Doctor Ro—" Her eyes widened as she cupped her hand over her own mouth.

"Who?" Hampton squinted.

Margot's face tightened.

Lucille slowly lowered her hand. "Doctor Parlimont is here." She chewed at the inside of her cheek and waited, in terror.

"Hampton? Hampton!" The deep voice echoed through one of the corridors.

"Why would the doorman let him in? No one was to enter…" Hampton muttered to himself.

Sara grimaced against the pain in her lower belly as she approached her husband and maids at the door. "Hamp, what's going on?"

"Sara! No, no. You *must* rest." Hampton grabbed her wrists then kissed the top of her head. "Lucille, usher Missus Parlimont to a seat. Margot, go feed the baby."

"Yes, sir." Young Lucille reluctantly reached up to place her hands on Sara's shoulders and guide her back into the suite.

Sara's heart was pounding. She could feel her blood pumping through her neck, temples, eyes, and arms. She was anxious to find out why he was in her home. She looked up to find Margot glaring at her.

"You'd better sit, Missus Parlimont," whispered Lucille. "You don't look well." She led the pale woman to a chaise lounge chair. Suckling sounds then caught Lucille's attention. She thought of her little brothers as she watched the baby nuzzle up against *her* mother.

"Hello… Bethiter to Lucille!" Sara waved her hands above her head.

Margot frowned.

"You weren't even listening, where you?" asked Sara.

Lucille's two pigtails swayed from side to side once she whipped her head in Sara's direction. "I'm sorry, Missus Parlimont. What did you say?"

"Did my father-in-law mention the reason for his visit?"

Outside of the nursery, Hampton wiped his palms along the sides of his pants then turned to his hefty bodyguard. "Stay here and keep watch, Ben. I'll be fine with James." He rested his hands on the rails of the stairwell and stared down at the black-and-white marble floor beneath him. For a fraction of a second, he wondered if it would mean sudden death if he threw his body over the railing head-first…as that's the only way he'd actually jump.

Chapter Four: Thirty-Four Years Prior on the Old World

When the time came for the top families to pick their new planets, it became increasingly difficult and caused a lot of friction, since some of the planets were obviously more ideal than others. After countless meetings and arguments over the subject, everyone decided that it would be most fair to have a monkey pull family names out of a hat. As fate would have it, the monkey died the morning of the drawing. Since they had no extra monkeys, someone jokingly suggested that Dr. Hampton Parlimont's one-year-old son was the next best thing.

So out they brought young Hampton, Jr. A few monkey sounds could be heard, which caused an outbreak of laughter. Dr. Parlimont, who'd become immune to being the butt off their jokes, sat back smugly in his wheelchair. Although he was brash, selfish, and cold-hearted, he was also one of the wealthiest men in the room.

The ten family names were tossed and shuffled a few times more, and a random, inhabitable planet was displayed on a large projector screen. Little Hampton then pulled a name. And that's how the matches were determined, one by one.

Chapter Five: Parlimont Manor II

Hampton stared down at the black–and–white marble floor beneath him.

"JUNIORRRR!" cracked the voice with impatience.

He grabbed a mint from his pocket, placed it on his tongue, and descended the staircase. His sweaty palm squeaked against the railing. By the time his loafer touched the floor, Hampton was approached by an old man, who was sitting in a motorized wheelchair. He'd brought three men with him. James, Hampton's bodyguard, swiftly placed his body before Hampton's and blocked the old man.

"It's alright," whispered Hampton. He then moved around James' massive frame and extended his hand to the visitor. "Hello, father."

"What the hell?" retorted the old man. The man's right eye was cloudy and sightless.

"Excuse me?"

"Is that all you have to say? 'Hello, father'? You have not seen me in years, yet you treat me this way," Doctor Parlimont scoffed. "Get me a drink!"

Hampton glanced above toward the nursery. He wanted to ensure that his curious wife hadn't escaped from the maids. "To the cigar lounge." He tilted his head in the direction of the elevator.

The household butler stood far behind the old man and his entourage. Hampton motioned for him to join them.

"Forgive me, sir," he whispered with a guilty expression; for, it was he (not the doorman) who'd opened the door for the unexpected visitors.

"It's quite alright, Steddy. He was bound to show eventually," Hampton assured.

Back in the nursery, Lucille and Margot nervously watched Sara pace back and forth. She blew her curly hair away from her face and bit her bottom lip until she tasted blood. Her tired eyes scanned Margot, who was still nursing the baby. The infant's tiny hand rested on Margot's ample, veiny breast. A ripple of defeat sank from Sara's chest to her toes. That was *her* baby.

"You can't go on like this. You have just given birth!" Margot urged.

"Is she latching, properly?" Sara questioned. Her shaky voice sounded as though she would burst into hysterics at any second.

"Yes." Margot gently stroked the newborn's cheek.

"Do suppose she's getting enough?"

"Yes. You will worry yourself sick. Lucille, make her sit."

Sara wiped her nose with the collar of her robe then turned to the young maid.

"Perhaps he has come with a solution. Perhaps he has found a cure. Do you think he knows I had the baby? Do you think that we have a spy? Maybe there is a traitor here!"

A bewildered Lucille looked to Margot for guidance. Using only her eyes, Margot warned her daughter not to respond to any of the roping questions. Sara understood their silent conversation and turned her face to the wall in frustration. She was nearly overcome with emotion. Her engorged breasts were heavy and sore. She'd packed her brassiere with cabbage leaves so that her milk supply would decrease, as the doctor had ordered. But the leaves didn't seem to be working this time. This fourth time. She wondered why things were the way they were. *Why couldn't she nurse her own baby? Why would God see fit to bless her with such a perfect baby... three to be specific... and take them all back within a week's time? Would her milk truly poison her child?* It was such a cruel and evil trick to play, she thought, to give one party riches and the other one life. *Who needs riches anyhow?*

"Lucille!" Sara exclaimed. "Find them and learn what he wants!"

This was the last thing that either maid wanted to hear.

"Have you lost your mind?" said Margot. "You can't be serious!" She rose and approached Sara.

"Do you have a better idea? If not, do your job!" Sara snapped.

Lucille saw a fire behind the mistress' eyes and somehow produced the courage to accept the assignment. She didn't want to upset her boss or see her mother get into any trouble. So, she took a deep breath and turned to leave.

"No, wait!" Sara blurted. Realizing that this task weighed heavily on the girl, she thought for a moment then quickly sat to remove her bloodstained panties and padding and wrapped them with a towel. "Take this... to the linen room." She handed the bundle to Lucille. "Thank you," she mustered.

"No!" Margot detached the baby from her breast. "How dare you risk the safety of *my* child? Lucille, stay here!"

"Lucille, do as I say!" Sara's blue eyes pierced through Margot.

"I don't want her to go."

"You have no say-so in the matter."

"And what if I were to throw your baby out of the window? Could you imagine?"

"What did you just say to me?" Sara sneered. "Unless you prefer that the two of you go home... permanently, I suggest you seal your damn lips and do as I say- when I say!"

Margot lowered her eyes and returned to her seat. She was ashamed of her lack of control and inability to protect her daughter.

"It's alright, mother." It wasn't. "I'm not afraid." She was. Lucille gave a pathetic attempt at a smile; but, was so nervous that she could barely grip the door handle to leave. Her hands shook terribly, and her stomach knotted to the point that she wished to curl up into a ball on the floor or die even. Nevertheless, she took a deep breath, raised her chin, and exited the nursery.

"Hey now… Where do you think you're going, little lady?" Ben said to Lucille as he continued to survey the area with his strikingly unique, ice-blue eyes.

Lucille stepped closer to the burly bodyguard and unwrapped the towel to expose the soiled underwear.

Ben quickly turned away. "Oh," he said. "Washroom? Be quick about it."

Lucille balled up the towel and scurried down the stairs.

"I need to go home now," Margot voiced as she lifted the sleeping baby from her breast and placed her over her shoulder. Her hazel eyes sliced Sara Parlimont into a thousand pieces.

"Oh, right…*your* babies. How old are they now?"

Margot hesitated. Suddenly she felt queasy. Her throat tightened. "The… twins are a week old today," she answered. Margot lightly patted the baby's back until she burped; then returned her to the crib.

Sara's eye twitched as she turned away from Margot. "Isn't that funny? How I lose three, and you get three." A hot tear dropped from her eye and down the corner of her lips. She peered out the large window in an opposite side of the room. The moonlight made her look even more beautiful than usual. The silver glow hid her red cheeks and heavy eyes. She was honestly surprised each time her eyes produced a tear because she figured that at some point, they would run out of salt and water.

Margot waited for the appropriate moment to leave without seeming heartless; although, she desperately missed her twin boys and knew that they were hungry. She was even more so concerned about Lucille. She detested Sara for putting her family in such a treacherous position. But what could she do? After considering her options, she made her way toward the doors.

"Do you think he knows?" asked Sara, still looking out the window into the dark.

"Who?! Mister Parlimont? Doctor Parlimont? How would I know?!"

Neither woman faced the other. There they stood. Both afraid. Both too proud to express their fear.

"You know, I too, have some in me. My great-great-grandfather was from—"

"That is not enough! That just won't do! You know that. Why would you ever place such a burden on me? Why?!" Margot straightened her back and stood tall.

Sara stared at the maid with her mouth open in shock.

"I will return in a couple of hours." Margot quickly exited the nursery and closed the door behind her.

Below in the cigar lounge, Hampton gulped down another glass of cognac as his father looked on in disgust. Then he lit his cigar and avoided looking at anyone. He knew that his father felt that drinking alcohol made a man weak, and that a weak man served no purpose. He would have rather had his father express his dismay instead of silently judging him. Hampton finished his drink and released a long, hot breath from his nose. He placed his empty tulip glass next to his father's full one and wondered why his father always asked for a drink… considering he had never seen him take a single sip of even champagne during toasts. But there had to be a reason. Hampton was convinced that there was a reason for everything that his father decided to do. As a young boy, his father would tell him how he gained success and established himself as one of the most powerful men in the Old World. For he believed that if surviving required everything, then one had better be prepared to lose it all.

"Don't you dare!" scolded Dr. Parlimont.

"Pardon me?" Hampton almost laughed in his father's face. He'd forgotten where they were. But they were in *his* home. "Why are you here?"

"Don't touch my drink." Dr. Parlimont wiped the sides of his mouth with his handkerchief and tucked it back into his blazer's front pocket. "I see you eyeing it."

A slight buzzing sound could be heard while he pressed a button on his left armrest. Slowly, his chair (and body) began to unfold. The buzzing and unfolding continued until Dr. Parlimont was standing upright. Two of his muscle men quickly knelt before him to straighten his crooked legs. Parlimont cleared his throat and smiled to himself.

"What would that be, son? Glass three? Four?" He peered down at his son.

Hampton Jr. stared at the floor.

"A glass for each dead baby I suppose," sighed Dr. Parlimont as he glided toward the bar. "Get him some water, boy," he said to Steddy, the butler.

"I don't want any water," Hampton snarled.

"The funny thing about 'want' is that 'need' always wins. Take the water."

Steddy was now holding a glass of water and standing between the father and son. He despised Dr. Parlimont and everything that he represented. The three bulky bodyguards stared at Steddy while Steddy stared at Hampton. Dr. Parlimont scowled, then threw his arm in a swift motion as if he expected the butler to force the water down Hampton's throat.

An uninvited pair of eyes looked on from a far corner of the room. In order to avoid the second guard, who stood watch in front of where the men were meeting, young Lucille crawled through a trap door in the linen room that led to another trap door in the cigar lounge. She'd cracked the door just enough so that she could see and hear what was happening. She was panting so hard that she feared they might hear her. She leaned forward until her forehead touched the doorframe. She feared for her safety and prayed for Steddy, her dear great-uncle, as tension filled the lounge. She'd heard plenty about Dr. "Robot" Parlimont and worried that his muscle men might hurt the old man. But Steddy showed no fear. Patiently, he waited.

"Take the water!" Dr. Parlimont boomed.

Hampton shook his head in disbelief; but then looked up into Steddy's kind, lonely face and knew that taking the glass of water was in the best interest of everyone there. He truly loved Steddy like a father, so he submitted.

"Thank you, Steven. That will be all," Hampton said as he accepted the glass.

Steddy bowed his head and returned to the bar. The three bodyguards taunted him as he passed by.

"How is my granddaughter?" Dr. Parlimont said with satisfaction while he watched Hampton sip from the glass like a pouting child.

"She is well. She is perfect."

"You mean… so far."

Hampton felt as if someone had given him a mighty blow to his gut. As much as he hated the words that his father had just spoken, Hampton was aware of their hostile reality. For no child born of a Pasturage family lived past a week.

"Have a seat, son." Dr. Parlimont dramatically drove his chair around the room and ended in front of the trap door. Lucille held her breath.

"Son, I realize that you have kept your distance from me due to misunderstandings." He secretly relished the thought of having his son's undivided attention. He hadn't seen him in more than five years.

"No, I have kept my family away from you because of the truth."

"*Whose* truth?! Tell me! Do not shut me out! Do not push me away! You are my son… A Parlimont. Your bloodline carries power and weight! Therefore, certain rules need not apply."

"You really *are* crazy," sneered Hampton.

Dr. Parlimont glanced at Steddy then smacked his lips. He knew that Hampton would never talk to him in private. The father and son began to argue immediately. Dr. Parlimont's feeble body squirmed in its awkward, upright position as his face turned red and his legs went crooked. Thick saliva collected in the corners of his mouth while he wagged his finger at his son. The underweight man threw a brief tantrum then wiped the sweat from his sun-spotted bald head. Hampton Jr. stood to leave.

Steddy looked on from behind the bar and wondered how such a small man could destroy so many healthy lives. *Does he feel no remorse? How has he not died from his own toxicity?* Steddy thought. He rubbed his tired hands against one another and fiddled with the golden wedding band around his ring finger. Thoughts of his wife still left him shattered after so many years. The two had met at a church picnic nearly forty years prior, during one of the hottest summers he'd ever felt. He closed his eyes and longed to smell the hearty smoke from that barbeque pit once again.

Chapter Six: Forty Years Prior in a Place Called Georgia

Steven Theodore Watters had led a drastically different life in the Old World. He had been a successful professional football player and public figure during his younger years.

"I'm so glad you decided to come out and join us common folk, Steddy!" joked Corrine, his older sister, as they hugged.

Children's laughter and barbeque smoke filled the air. Music played.

"Oh whatever, sis. You know it's not like that. I've just been busy. Man it's a lot of folks out here today!"

"Yeah... *busy*. Who's it this time? Miss Keep ya Busy: the blonde swimsuit model? Or Miss Keep ya Busy: your teammate's ex-wife? Oh, how 'bout Miss Keep ya Busy: the weather girl slash stalker-chick, who popped up at momma's flower shop last Valentine's Day?"

"Damn, sis. Don't do me like that!"

Corrine punched Steddy in the shoulder. He flexed his arm and laughed.

"Sted! Boy… Watch your mouth! Come on around this way. Pete's over there on the grill. And the rest of the guys are down at the lake fishing. Everybody's gonna be so glad to see you!"

"Ah… sure smells good, Reenie-Bear. Is ol Pete ready for fatherhood?"

"He better be! 'Cause my little Margot is coming regardless!"

"I know that's right!"

They laughed and chatted as they approached the church members.

"That's our new Pastor and First Lady, over there, Sted. I'll introduce you. Hold on one sec, though… Hey, Pete! Who made the potato salad? You know I don't eat everybody's potato salad!" Corrine sighed as she fanned herself with a paper plate. She was out of breath and already tired of the heat. "And remind me to never be summer-time pregnant again!"

Smiling faces and loving salutations met Steddy as he passed by his hometown church members. He was overcome with joy.

"Feels good to be home," he said to himself. He looked around and wondered how life would've turned out if he'd never left that small, country town.

The *clank! clank!* of horseshoes being tossed could be heard. The youth choir was playing volleyball. Deacon Tisdel was sitting beneath the shade of a tree while he strummed his guitar. Listeners rocked from side-to-side and sang along. The Mother's Board was in charge of the cakewalk. They had pecan pie, sweet potato pie, buttermilk pie, peach cobbler, pound cake, upside-down cake, and Mother Strother's famous banana cake. Sitting behind the cake table was a stunning, caramel-skinned woman wearing stylish sunglasses. Her long, shiny black hair danced in the summer breeze as a few strands slid across her lips. She was content. Not talking to anyone. Not playing any games.

Steddy's feet stopped moving. "Hold up… Who's that, sis?"

"Who's who?" Corrine asked while she inspected the potato salad and baked beans. "Pete! Who made the baked beans this year?"

"Corrine, who is *that*? Over there, behind the cake table." Steddy tapped his sister's arm and licked his lips.

"Who?" Corrine turned her head toward the cakewalk. "Oh, uh uh! N and a big fat O. Nope! No sir. Not gonna happen. That's the Pastor's daughter. She just got back from studying abroad in Italy. She's a good girl, Sted. Leave that one alone. Hey, Pete! Honey, come get your brother-in-law. I'm too hungry for this nonsense."

"Yo, Steddy Sted! What's going on man?" Pete asked as he handed his wife a frosty jar of sweet tea. He removed his sooty apron and offered his hand to Steddy for a shake. "Hot enough out here for you, bro? Your sister's about to drive me crazy, man. Aye… Sted? You alright? Hey…"

She was the most beautiful woman he had ever seen. It was if God had handcrafted this woman at the beginning of time, for this precise moment. Steddy went deaf. He went breathless. He didn't want to stop looking at her for even a second. He felt nothing but the desire to be near her. It scared him to feel that way; but he wanted nothing less. And after that day, they were never apart.

Steddy Watters invested wisely and after his football career, became the owner of more than dozen dry cleaning businesses and two-dozen laundromats. With the help of his wife, Julia, Steddy birthed an array of lucrative small businesses for his family and close friends. They all flourished with multiple businesses and organizations that would have ensured financial security for many generations to follow had not the "big move" occurred.

On the night of Steddy's fortieth birthday, he received an alarming call from his attorney. He rushed to his bedroom to find his wife and five-year-old son asleep.

Ten families. Ten planets. That was the goal. To allow each top family to transfer the richest, smartest, healthiest, and most attractive of "their" land; and start a world anew.

Chapter Seven: Parlimont Manor III

"For Christ's Sake, Junior! Hear me!" pleaded an exhausted Dr. Parlimont. "I can *save* her!"

Hampton froze. He then slowly removed his hand from the doorknob and looked over his shoulder.

Steddy's eyes filled with tears as he listened to Dr. Parlimont share his discoveries with his son. "Robot" Parlimont spared no twisted detail with his explanation of his whereabouts, despicable experiments, and shocking solution with his son. And even more unbelievable was the fact that the drunken Hampton seemed to be intrigued by what his father had to say.

"How do you think I've made it this far, son?" Dr. Parlimont caught his breath. He then fixed his gaze upon his son as he unbuttoned his shirt to expose a thick, brown scar that ran down the middle of his bony chest. The room sat still as everyone looked on in amazement. "This is my third transplant."

Dr. Robot's vile speech and the sight of his repulsive scar was more than poor Lucille could bear. She gagged then cupped her hand over her mouth to keep from vomiting. Quickly, she scooted out of the small space between the cigar lounge and linen room and was overcome with relief the moment her feet touched the floor. She turned to dart toward the nearest exit but found herself nose-to-bosom with Garla Lastoré, Parlimont Manor's third maid.

Garla was a strikingly gorgeous, young woman, who always wore the expression of someone who'd tasted rancid meat. Her mother was an international socialite on Earth and was rumored to have been one of Dr. Parlimont's "special" friends. Her dying wish was to be guaranteed that her only child would make it to Bethiter. In true Dr. Robot fashion, he accepted the woman's multimillion-dollar "good-faith" investment, and treated Garla as the help her entire life. However, she was not much of a maid and spent most of her time flirting with the men of the estate.

"Now what sort of rat is *this*?" hissed Garla with her hands on her hips.

"I-I-I was loading Missus Parlimont's dirty clothes into the washer." Lucille's eyes were as large as two full moons. She was so afraid that her entire body began to tremble.

"A big rat. A big, brown, *sneaky* rat!"

"Please, Garla... I was just leav—"

"*Miss* Garla!" she snapped. "Hasn't your mother taught you anything about respect?"

"Miss Garla, please, I'm begging you. I just want to go home."

"And it speaks! My word! When I thought I'd seen everything under the sphere, I run into a talking rat!" Garla snickered and bumped into the petrified young girl as she walked further into the linen room. "What were you doing in here?"

"I was washing clothes. Missus Parlimont asked me to do it."

The muffled voices of Dr. Parlimont and Hampton could be heard. Garla peered into the washing machine and lifted the bloody panties.

"No water. No soap. You were eavesdropping!" Garla threw the garments at Lucille's face and wiped her hands on her apron. "So, come on... out with it!"

"Huh?"

"Don't play stupid with me. What did the sneaky rat learn while hiding in here? Tell me!"

Just then, a sturdy knock startled them both.

"Oh, Ben! You almost made me jump out of my flesh!" exclaimed Garla.

"Is everything alright? I came down to check on Lucille. Did you take care of that...um... issue?" Ben, still holding his gun, tilted his head toward the front door. "You better be getting home. Your mother will begin to worry. She doesn't need that."

"Yes. Yes! Thank you," whispered a tearful Lucille. She slid by Garla and scurried out of the linen room toward the front door.

Garla swore to herself.

"Did you say something?" Ben asked. He quickly admired Garla's curves from top to bottom. "Why are the clothes on the floor?"

Garla stared at him for a moment and wondered how such a dark-skinned person could have light, blue eyes. Then she considered how grand it would be if their features collaborated and produced a child. She smiled at the thought of her olive skin and pouty lips with his high cheekbones and bright eyes. "How tall are you, again, Benjamin?" Garla purred as she approached the muscular bodyguard. "Every time I see you, I could swear you have gotten... bigger."

Ben poked his chest out and stepped closer to the lovely temptress.

"I can let you be the judge of that Miss Garla. But how will you measure? I don't see a ruler."

"Oh, I'm sure we can find a way..."

Chapter Eight: The Crowd

The Community hadn't seen Grate in sixteen years. After Dr.
Parlimont continued to pass laws that oppressed the commoners, the

king (before he was king) attempted to rally everyone and lead an insurgency. Regrettably, members of The Pasturage had no incentive to revolt and those of The Community were too afraid of the consequences. Conversely, the indigenous human-like creatures that he and his grandmother had come to trust were ready for war. And that's how they earned the name 'Surges'.

"Are you sure? Can it be? Is he really here?" a Community woman excitedly asked her younger sister.

"Yes! It's true! I hear that he's taller than a vumble tree... and far more handsome than anyone could ever describe. Here, wear *this* blouse. It complements your figure," the sister replied. She bounced with joy and clapped her hands.

The woman ran a red clay mixture across her lips with the tip of her finger and lightly tapped her cheeks for color.

"You look perfect! He will want to marry you on sight!" said the little sister.

"Thank you. I do feel queenly." She brought her long hair to one side and over her shoulder before placing a flower behind her ear. "But we must be clever. I need a reason to approach Godmother's den so that I may see him face-to-face."

They both thought for a moment.

"Here! Take father's mint salve that he bought from the market."

"But this is the last of it. Do you think he'll mind?"

"Does it matter? This is the *king*!"

The sisters hurried from their lodge toward the Godmother's den and were stunned to discover the massive crowd that had gathered in the area.

"I'm going to make my way through. Stay here," the woman told her sister. Next, she turned to weave through the mass. She ignored the shoves, cursing, and even pinches from bystanders, and continued to march forward. She stretched her neck to see how far she was from the den and there it was!

And there *they* were. The windows and front door were being guarded by Surges.

"The cave-people are real?!" The young woman released the jar from her hands in astonishment. It broke at her feet.

Past the multitude of people, loyal Surges, and rust-colored walls, was the home of the Godmother. She was The Community's eldest and most respected member. Although her physical body was frail, her spirit was strong and maintained its power. Her wavy, gray hair fell to the small of her back. She walked with a large, crooked stick that she'd brought from the Old World and spent the majority of her time outside meditating or exploring the planet. She'd found herbs and stones that were useful remedies for common ailments and discovered a way to produce fruits and vegetables from the strange Bethiter soil. These efforts saved countless families from starvation and certain illnesses during difficult seasons. Her grasps on the wonders of both the natural and spiritual worlds and clever sense of humor made her a refreshing force to be near. Dr. Parlimont was convinced that she was senile and left her alone to do as she pleased.

"Excuse me." The young woman tapped her neighbor's shoulder. "What is going on?"

"Godmother has taken ill," answered a stout man. "She collapsed earlier while praying in the valley and has yet to awaken." After noticing how attractive the woman was, he stepped closer to her and brushed his mustache with his fingertips.

"How dreadful! So that is why the king has come."

"KEEEEEP BAAAAACK!" shouted a colossal Surge, who was protecting the front door.

The crowd stood still and fell quiet at the sound of the giant's incredibly powerful voice. It vibrated through them and lingered in the air. To the young woman's delight, she'd reached the front of the crowd. She wondered what the king was doing that very moment.

Chapter Nine: Godmother's Den

Godmother's den was dark and calm. A soothing peace swaddled the place. Although the floors were dirt and the ceiling was made of straw, the home was immaculate. It seemed as if the den possessed the freshest air and carried the sweetest aromas. Various stones that had been found in The Stretch's valleys and forbidden caves illuminated the room. The Godmother was the king's grandmother on his father's side.

The king stood over her and watched her sleep. He couldn't believe that so much time had passed since he'd been there. When he'd gotten word that she had fallen into some sort of unknown sleep, he and several of his mightiest warriors immediately traveled to The Community to be by her side.

Fascinatingly, twenty-three years prior, their roles were in reverse and it was he, who was on his deathbed in this same room.

"I will not give up on you, Momma," King Grate whispered.

Chapter Ten: Twenty-Three Years Prior on Bethiter

"What's going on with my nephew?" Corrine asked. She sat in a rocking chair by the front door and wondered if masks should be worn.

"It's been three days and he hasn't stirred," said a nurse as she placed a cool towel across a sleeping boy's forehead.

"There's nothing left to do. This sickness is unknown to us and the fever won't break. He must be quarantined," gave a remorseful doctor, who'd been monitoring the boy.

"Wait a minute. Repeat that, doc." Corrine stood.

"His grandmother won't let him go. You know that," whispered the nurse.

"Why is everyone so afraid of her?" the doctor replied. "We don't know what we're dealing with here or if it's contagious. The patient must be isolated. I believe we should do so before the old woman returns." The doctor washed his hands in a large bowl that sat on a table at the foot of the bed.

"That *old woman* is my mother and *the patient* is my nephew! If you feel the need to be disrespectful, there's the door." Corrine folded her arms and waited for the doctor's response.

Suddenly, Steddy charged into the room. The doctor jumped back and caused the bowl of water to topple to the floor. Steddy was gasping for air and drenched with sweat. He looked at young Grate and dropped to his knees once he realized that the boy was still breathing. He then began to sob uncontrollably. The nurse tossed a dry rag to the doctor before rushing to comfort him.

"Shhhhh, Steddy. Pull yourself together. We must not alarm The Community," she said as she rocked him in her arms.

Corrine joined them and tried to console her brother.

The annoyed doctor dabbed himself with the rag. "Right. We must not alarm The Community any more than we *already* have. Grate will be moved to another part of the planet today."

"Another part of the planet?" Steddy rose to his feet. He was almost a foot taller than the doctor.

"Relax, Sted. Just hold on." Corrine held his arm. "Stay calm, bro."

"He's going." The doctor gulped and straightened his back. "The decision has been made."

Corrine released her brother.

"You mean you've decided to let my little boy die?! My only child?? And run off with my money, huh? What sort of doctor are you anyhow? You... you crook!" With that, he sprang toward the doctor and wrapped his large hands around his neck.

"No, stop!" screamed the nurse as she jumped onto Steddy's wide back.

"Get off of him! Get down!" yelled Corrine.

Members of The Community began to approach the den and peek through the windows.

"Be... STILL!" roared a pained voice.

Steddy, the doctor, the nurse, and Corrine looked in the direction of the front door and scrambled to stand upright.

"They're going to let him die—"

"There is nothing left for us to do!"

"He attacked him and I couldn't just stand and watch—"

"Leave! All of you!" Gave the woman as she turned to the spectators, who had surrounded her home. "You should all be ashamed of yourselves! Every last one of you!"

"Forgive me, Godmother," the doctor uttered as he bowed and hobbled out of the room.

"Please, I never meant to disrespect your space, Godmother. Please— thank you," wept the nurse once she'd reached the exit.

"You too, Reenie. Let me talk to Sted."

Corrine nodded and followed the nurse.

The proud matriarch approached the boy and removed the towel from his brow. She then picked up the broken washbowl from the floor and placed it back onto the table.

"Where have you been, son?" she asked while facing the window.

"I... I went to see Doctor Parlimont," Steddy replied as he dusted himself off and straightened his clothing.

"You went to see that maniac?!"

Steddy dropped his head.

"And...?"

"And he refused to see my boy. All he gave me was this damned concoction!" He removed a tube from his pocket and threw it across the room.

"Get out of here with Parlimont's poison!"

"I was desperate. I can't lose him, momma. I'd go crazy. I'd die right along with him!" Steddy dropped to his knees and crawled to his mother.

"Rise to your feet! You are a man! This will not defeat you. Up!" The old woman shook her head in disappointment and approached her dying grandson. She touched his little feet then paused. "Steddy, what price did you pay for that elixir?"

He covered his face with his hands and began to weep.

"Son?" she sat on the bed and braced herself.

"I'm too ashamed to say."

"Answer me. I know nothing comes cheap from that devil."

"I'm going to be… the help," Steddy said through clenched teeth. "I'll live and work in his home… as his butler."

"As his what?! His butler? Have you gone completely insane?"

"I didn't know what else to do!"

"You've spent a year away from him already. You just got out. And now you leave him for good?!" She rose to her feet and pointed her walking stick at the door. "Leave then!! Leave now! And take Parlimont's sorry medicine with you!"

Once alone, the old woman began to remove the strips of cloth that were wrapped around her feet and ankles. After three days of walking through the valley, her feet were cracked and beaten. Her open wounds were garnished with bits of grass, dirt, and thread. She flinched in pain as she tugged at shredded pieces of cloth that were stuck to her bloody feet. She rested for a moment; then from her bosom retrieved a vial of what appeared to be bright pink water. She carefully opened it and allowed a drop of it to fall onto each section of ripped flesh. The Godmother moaned in pain as the pink liquid foamed and crackled on her skin. She wiped sweat from beneath her nose and exhaled a long sigh of relief. Her torn and calloused feet had transformed into smooth, healthy ones.

She turned to her grandson and smiled. Gently, she cradled the boy's head with one hand and opened his mouth with the other. As with her feet, the pink nectar popped and fizzled upon touching his lips. She poured it into his mouth, over his eyes, and allowed it to run down the sides of his face. Immediately, his color began to return. His lips twitched. And his labored breathing began to calm.

"Grate, you are a king," she whispered. Tears of triumph streamed down her face. "You are not like the others. And I'll never give up on you!"

Chapter Eleven: Family

Without a minute wasted, Lucille fled with all of her might to The Community. She ran even faster once her cabin was in sight and leapt over the front stairs and directly onto the porch. She was so grateful to see her mother that all she could do was cry. Margot had been kneeling in prayer next to her bed. Up she sprang to comfort her wheezing daughter once the door opened.

"Lucille?! Darling! What have they done to you? Did they hurt you?"

"Oh, mommy it's horrible! Far worse than anyone could imagine! No child younger than five is safe!" she whimpered.

A sharp pain struck the middle of Margot's chest as Lucille recited Dr. Parlimont's speech. Margot fell back onto the wall; as she was close to fainting.

"I'm so scared!" Lucille fell into her mother's arms.

"Have you told anyone else?"

"No. I came straight here."

"My sweet, sweet babies. I can't lose them!" Margot slowly looked around the room and thought of a plan. Next, she yanked her cloak from its hook on the wall and wrapped it around herself.

"Mom?"

"Stay here and don't let anyone in! I'm getting help!"

After ten minutes of walking through the dark community, Margot reached the outer perimeter that hosted the Godmother's den. She squinted then slowed her pace. "Surges?!"

"Halt!" boomed the Surge's powerful voice. "State your purpose!"

"I-I have come to see Grate! And my grandmother. I am the daughter of *her* daughter," answered Margot. She couldn't believe how big he was. She looked down at his enormous hands and feet and wondered how often he bathed. She attempted to smile at him, but he only looked straight ahead.

Moments later, the front door of Godmother's den opened, and the doorkeeper stepped aside to reveal a smaller Surge.

"State your purpose," said Argan, the king's defender.

Margot was relieved to see a less intimidating cave dweller. She relaxed some and stepped forward.

"Well, I have already explained—"

Argan rolled her eyes and shut the door right away. Soon after, the giant Surge returned to his initial position. Margot stared at him in amazement. She couldn't believe how rude the creatures were behaving. She wondered if yelling loudly enough would make her cousin come outside. They hadn't seen each other in fifteen or sixteen years. It's amazing to consider how much a relationship can change over the course of time. The two were extremely close as children. They were more like siblings really. And now, she was waiting for the permission to merely see him. She remembered the day he was born and how happy everyone was. There were so many toothy smiles and long, cozy hugs. At times it felt as though memories from The Old World were just dreams.

"State your purpose!" the Surge bellowed once again; but, with more agitation.

Margot fell to her hands and knees in terror. Her beating heart pained her as she struggled for air. Before now, she'd believed that the Surges were only fairytale creatures that were made up to keep The Community's children from exploring the planet.

"I have come to see my cousin!" Margot exclaimed. She wanted to add how urgent the matter was and that she was not the enemy.

The Surge huffed, then as before, moved aside just enough to expose the den's front door. Next, the front door creaked open to show the petite, yet fierce, Argan once again.

"State your purpose!" she ordered.

"The children of The Community are in danger! I must see Grate!" Margot cried. Mucous hung from her nose as she tried to keep control of her emotions. She gripped the soft clay beneath her hands.

"You may see the *king*. Come in," Argan said.

Margot rushed into the den. The room was inviting and still. She was grateful for such relief. Upon seeing the Godmother, she froze. For the first time ever, the old lady actually looked her age. She looked frail, weak, and helpless.

"Oh, Grandmother!" she whispered. She used a portion of her apron to wipe her nose and mouth.

"What brings you?" said the king. He sat behind her in a rocking chair, with Argan standing to his right.

"Grate! You startled me!"

"Why have you come?"

"Is it possible for you and me to speak in private, cousin?"

"No."

An embarrassed Margot composed herself and stood tall. "Very well then. I need your help. The Community needs your help. For years, Doctor Parlimont has been stealing our babies and children for experiments! And he plans to kidnap more. All because he wants to use our hearts to save their babies! I can't let him take my babies! I've given birth just a week ago. Surely they'd be at the top of his list," Margot's voice cracked. She looked to Argan for support but received none.

"I will have everyone in The Community relocated to the caves. There, you and your babies will be safe."

"What? No!" Margo shouted.

Argan hissed and her emerald eyes began to glow. Margot stepped back and bowed her head in apology.

"No?! Have you gone mad?" the king spat. "What right do you have to request my help; only to refuse it?"

Margot fiddled with her fingers and stared at the floor. "It's just that we are happy here—"

"Happy? Happy as slaves, wet-nurses, and bed wenches?"

"How dare you?" Margot growled. Her eyes met Argan's, then she softened her tone. "We are your family. Doesn't that mean anything to you anymore?"

"When's the last time you visited Grandmother before now? Or the last time you spoke with her or made sure that she'd eaten?"

Margot started to respond but couldn't. She was ashamed to consider the last few years. The Godmother was rumored to be demented and considered uncivilized by the "elite" members of The

Community. She'd refused to adapt to the ways of the New World, and for that reason had become an outcast as far as Margot was concerned.

"Did you ever wonder where she'd be during those long hours in the valley? Did you even care?" The king bit his fist in frustration. "She would be with *me*! Safe with me! My warriors would dig up roots for her medicines and find fruit and vegetables for her to return to all of you. The only reason she remained here is because The Community would perish without her. Fools!"

"I'm sorry! Please! Please!" Margot cried. She fell onto her knees and groveled. "He's going to kill our babies! He's found that our hearts are stronger than their own. He's going to transplant our babies' hearts into their babies' chests so that they'll live past a week! Countless mothers of The Community were told that their babies were stillborn; but it wasn't true. He stole them and experimented on them! Oh, God! He's even used the hearts for himself! What will become of us?" Margot grabbed her head and howled in dismay.

"My mind is unchanged. Come with me to the caves or stay here to meet your fate. Now, the time has come for you to leave," replied the king as he gazed upon his beloved grandmother and motioned for Argan to take Margot away.

"You are so egotistical and selfish!" Margot screeched. "You've always been a jerk! As if you're better than everybody else!"

Argan quickly grabbed her by the arm and began to drag her toward the door.

"No! No! No! Let me go, you trifling beast!" Margot fought by tossing her body from side to side in an attempt to escape the Surge's incredible hold. "Have you no soul, Grate?! What of our babies? What of *your* baby?!"

"Wait!"

Argan stared down at Margot in disgust.

"Release her," he said as he rose. "Repeat yourself."

"Which part?" Margot heaved while she rubbed her aching wrist. "Are you not aware that the new Parlimont baby's not truly a Parlimont?" Margot smirked as she stood. Blood ran down the insides of her legs. "Were you not aware?" she jeered. "Oh. Well, the secret's out. The king and the missus have created a love child!"

Argan's eyes began to change from emerald to scarlet.

"Hold your tongue," the king commanded.

Margot smiled. "And in a week's time, she will not die as all the others before have. That is, if she survives the heart operation."

"Say no more!"

"She will turn brown and her hair will coil…"

"Do as I command!" Grate stepped closer to his cousin.

"And everyone will know that the new princess is nothing but a bastard!"

"Silence!" roared the king as he slapped Margot across her face with the back of his hand. He turned to his grandmother for a moment, as if to apologize for the unrest, before returning to his seat.

"Do you think you're better than us?" Foam gathered in her mouth. She held her stinging cheek and continued to shout. "You're no better than anyone! You are nothing! Your own father deserted you!"

With that, Argan waved in Margot's direction, which caused her to lose consciousness and collapse onto the floor.

"Mommy! Mom, wake up! Please wake up!" Lucille cried as she shook Margot and splashed cold water on her face.

"Lucille?" she coughed. "Where… How did I get here?"

"A Surge brought you and placed you on the bed!"

"What?"

"A real, live Surge!"

Margot rubbed her face as she recalled the conversation with her cousin. "I must think of something else. Grate refuses to help us."

"Refuses? But we're family. Maybe the Surges can—"

"Quiet. I have a plan."

Still dazed, Margot prepared a week's worth of milk for her twin boys and packed it along with food for Lucille into a large leather-bark pouch. Then the two dressed the babies into layers of clothes.

"What happened to your face?"

"Shhhh... Grab your cloak."

Lucille struggled to keep her hands steady to button her cloak. She wondered what her mother was thinking. And if Surges were real, then what else was out there? She'd heard stories about the "rebel" king her entire life; and figured that he'd somehow overreacted. That maybe the zealous young leader was power hungry and too headstrong. She'd been taught to be grateful for Dr. Parlimont, as life wouldn't have been possible without him. He was to be respected and honored... never crossed.

Lucille gasped. "Mommy, you're bleeding!" She pointed down at Margot's feet.

"I'm fine."

"Your body hasn't healed. I'm worried about you."

"I said I'm fine. Come help me..."

Lucille dashed to her mother's side and lifted their heavy mattress from its frame with her.

"There! Grab the map."

The young girl did as she was told and retrieved an old folded piece of cloth. Margot snatched it from her and studied it.

"Put on the wrap. It is time to go." Margot embraced her boys before securing them in the sling that Lucille now wore. One in front and the other in back.

"Go?" Lucille's voice trembled.

So much had happened over the course of a week. Even though she was only eleven, Lucille started working at Parlimont Manor in her mother's place, because she'd given birth to the twins early. Then after strenuous labor, Margot was summoned from bed rest to care for Mrs. Parlimont and the new baby. Next, Dr. Robot appeared, unannounced and obviously unwelcome. Nothing was right anymore.

"Put your mind at ease, my love," offered Margot. "All will be well." With map in hand, she then explained where they should go. "Head for the Breathing Valley. Take this route," Margot licked her dry lips and fought back tears.

"The Stretch? You want us to go into The Stretch?!"

"There is no other way."

"Wait, who even gave you this map? How can we trust it? We will die out there!"

"Return in one week's time. And whatever you do, never drink the wild water!"

"Mommy!"

"Go, now! Hurry! I love you." Margot kissed her babies and hugged Lucille one last time, then guided Lucille out of the lodge. She held her breath as she watched her children fade into the darkness of the night.

She couldn't believe what was happening. She'd learned that she was pregnant just days after her husband's sudden death. Memories of the Old World played through her mind. She'd attended a prestigious private school and had dreams of becoming a veterinarian. Her family's home had three stories. With a fenced-in yard. And a piano. And a housekeeper named Agatha. She never would've imagined that *she'd* be someone's maid or nanny, yet alone wet-nurse. Once, her Uncle Steddy mentioned how women would get a month or so of "maternity leave" from work; after giving birth. Margot laughed to herself. When Mrs. Parlimont went into labor early that morning, Margot was forced out of bed.

Then she remembered the look in Sara's eyes after she gave birth. Pure terror overshadowed any signs of happiness as she held her new baby... her fourth child and first daughter.

"Margot, can you keep a secret?" she'd asked.

Margot washed her face and body. After changing into a clean dress and pair of shoes, she fixed her shiny chestnut hair into a tidy bun. Her meeting at the Godmother's had left her rather disheveled, not to mention sore. She took a shot of fermented valley-berry juice then kneeled beside her bed.

"...For Thou art with me," she prayed.

Chapter Twelve: The Baptism

Steddy answered the door upon Margot's arrival to the manor and was struck by an unfamiliar look in her eyes. Fear, astonishment, sadness, hopelessness, and confusion rested in their shadows. And... there was something else that he couldn't name.

"You alright, Margot?"

"Hey! Of course! I'm better than ever," she replied before kissing his cheek. "Isn't it past your bedtime? I'm surprised to see you awake, Uncle Sted."

"I was just brewing some tea to settle my stomach," answered Steddy. "Have some?"

"Goodnight!" Margot sang, ignoring his offer. She paused for a moment then began humming an old baptism tune that Steddy recognized from his childhood church.

He scratched his head and watched Margot prance away. He knew that her husband's death affected her immensely and worried about her mental health, not to mention her physical well-being. The silver spoon clanged against the bone china teacup as he stirred the tea and honey mixture. He sighed. It was such a beautiful prison; the Parlimont Manor. He was trapped in his skin, forever bound to a life of servitude -and of course, as a hostage of the sphere.

When Margot entered the nursery, she found Sara sitting on the floor, rocking back and forth. She was gray with worry.

"Margot! Oh, thank goodness! Where's Lucille? She never returned after going to the linen room. Please tell me she's alright! I called you, but you didn't answer."

"Yes, she is fine. Don't worry. Come, let me help you get into bed." Margot smiled and rested her hand on Sara's shoulder.

"I'm not tired. Are you alright?"

"Yes. How is the princess?"

Sara stared at Margot then crossed her arms. "What in the sphere is going on?"

"What do you mean?"

"What did Lucille say about Doctor Parlimont?"

"Not much. Same old Doctor Robot and his musings… New ideas and laws and whatnots."

"Excuse me? Robot?"

"You must be exhausted. You should go rest." Margot gently grabbed her shoulders and walked toward the door.

"Go? What do you mean go?" Sara quickly turned to face her and laughed at the thought.

"You won't be any good for this delicious baby if you don't rest and properly take care of yourself. Tell you what—"

"Stop. What did Lucille say? Why was he here?"

"Has he left?"

Sara nodded. "Hampton and the guards left with him an hour or so ago. I've been tormented by my own thoughts all the while." She released a failed attempt at a chuckle and then erupted into tears. "And you took so long…"

Margot embraced her and stroked her curly, red tresses. "Now, now. Shhhh. Go to your suite and lie down. Put your feet up and relax. You must rest."

"Oh, Margot," she said between sniffles. "I'm so afraid. There is something amiss."

"You're paranoid. Sleep deprivation will do that."

"Something's very wrong here. I can feel it!"

"Everything will be fine. You'll see. Go and get some sleep."

"Why do you keep telling me to go? I never leave my babies."

"You will worry yourself sick if you go on like this." Margot handed a soft blanket to a quivering Sara. "And what use would you be for her then? You must heal."

Sara thought for a moment. Her stomach felt as though a nest of snakes were wrestling inside. Her breasts were hard and swollen with milk. The cabbage definitely wasn't working. She'd spent the last five years pregnant. Pregnant and grieving. Pregnant and birthing and grieving and apologizing. Searching and praying and hoping and grieving. All of this without healing. *But how does one heal the soul?* she wondered. She approached the crib and looked down at her baby. Maybe Margot was right. It wasn't practical to stay cooped up in the nursery and be suffocated by her own anxiety. It probably wasn't good for the baby either.

"I've always wanted a daughter. And She's so beautiful. I really want her, Margot."

"She's fine. Go rest, *please*."

Sara nodded in agreement and prepared to leave the nursery. She kissed her index finger and placed it on the crown of the infant's fuzzy head.

Once alone, Margot slightly opened one of the nursery doors and scanned the halls. No one could be seen or heard. She was in a great deal of pain, both physically and emotionally. She could feel the blood escaping her body and soaking her padding. She walked over to the large window and wondered if she'd made the right decision by sending them away. Images of her courageous daughter and defenseless sons pushed their way to the forefront of her mind. They deserved a chance at life as much as anyone else. What other choice did she have?

The baby began to cry.

"You must be hungry. Shhh, poor thing!" Margot carried the baby from her crib and began to hum the same tune as before. She nursed her as she limped to the bathroom. "Did you know that your room is bigger than my family's entire home?" She plugged the tub and turned the ivory faucet knob on the bathtub. "But that's not your fault. None of this is. You poor, innocent thing. I'm sorry that your silly parents placed you in the middle of this predicament. You still smell like the angels but are causing a lot of hell for us right now. So, I'm going to return you to God so that your cousins may live their lives the way He intended." She then placed the baby into the rising water.

Sara sat up in her bed. She rubbed her belly and realized that she missed being pregnant. There'd been Hampton the Third, Hampton Nicholas, Hampton Brooks, and... this one. She hadn't expected the baby to be a girl or taken the time to consider a name. Without provocation, she thought of Grate. His wisdom and deliberate ways about everything. His soft, comforting eyes and hard, strong hands. His chiseled jawline and shy dimples. His long, muscular torso…

Unexpectedly, a spine-tingling scream tore through the halls.

"Margot?!" Sara jumped from her position and clumsily made her way toward the nursey.

Steddy was reaching the top of the stair-case as Sara passed. Then, the nursery doors flung open. It was Margot and her hair had turned stark white!

"Margot??" Steddy could hardly speak.

"Margot, where's the baby? Margot?!" Sara cried as she ran with all her might.

"That bastard is *not* of God! She came here to destroy us all!" Sara pushed Margot to the side and darted into the nursery.

"Good Lord, what have you done?" Steddy begged through a whisper.

"I- I- She… She will be the death of us all…" Margot began to pray, then speak gibberish. Strings of drool hung from her mouth as she clawed her face until vertical lines of ripped flesh appeared. She smiled.

Steddy slowly approached her, with his arms out in surrender. "Margot. What have you done? Talk to me."

"I must go," she laughed. "I've got to get out of here. Will you stay with this whore and your granddaughter or finally come home where you belong?"

Steddy went rigid.

"Gratey knows! He knows what he's done. And he hit me, Uncle Sted!" Margot continued to scratch her face. "Plus, your mother is dying," she said with her pointer finger in the air. "Ohhh! Today has just been full of surprises hasn't it?" She threw her head back in laughter and descended the winding staircase. Her incoherent babbling continued as she walked out the front door.

Steddy stood in place. He was bewildered and afraid. "Missus Parlimont?" he said after a moment. He knocked on the nursery door but heard nothing. Slowly, he entered the suite. Everything was in its place. Then he heard noises coming from the bathroom and quickly advanced that way. There he found Sara on the floor, nursing her naked baby.

"Margot tried to drown her," she tearfully reported. However, a hint of pride shone in her eyes. This was her first time ever nursing.

"Is it true, Serenity?"

"What?"

"Is it true? Is this my son's child?"

Sara's eyes filled with tears as she mouthed 'yes'. Steddy turned to leave.

"No, it's not what you think! Let me explain—" Sara attempted to stand but struggled to find her balance.

"You claimed you were out there seeking help from my mother! I trusted you. I *lied* for you!" Steddy threw his hands up in disbelief.

Just then, commotion could be heard in the foyer.

"They're back! Help me… please!" Sara swiftly removed the baby from her breast and readjusted her robe. "Wait, I've got to show you something."

"I don't want to hear or see anything from you! They will kill my son as well as me! Do you understand? My God! You have no clue!" He gently helped her to her feet and peeked toward the nursery exit.

"No, Mister Watters! You have to see!" Sara walked to the bathtub.

"I'm leaving. My mother is ill and tonight might be the last for the both of us."

"Just look!" With that, Sara released her newborn into the water.

"Have you completely lost it too?!" Steddy rushed to save the baby. But stopped mid-step.

Gill-like slits had appeared along the infant's rib cage! Slowly, they opened and closed, exposing feathery red organs and providing the baby with oxygen. The baby ran her balled fist across her lips until she found her thumb to use as a pacifier. A wide smile formed on Steddy's face; the type of smile that only comes out for special occasions. He hadn't smiled that way in a very long time.

Chapter Thirteen: Unrequited Love and Grate Dreams

After learning that no one and nothing was off limits to Dr. Robot, King Grate knew that it was best that they return to The Stretch. One of the Surges held the inert Godmother, as they traveled on the backs of giant sea swallows through the brilliant, dark wilderness. Every inch of the black ground flirted with any sign of light and glimmered new colors never seen on earth. The plants curiously watched them pass by. The Living Pools flowed next to them. They giggled and played tag with themselves… because on Bethiter, the water was a group of many things and never just one.

"What worries you, my Lord?" Argan asked. "King? …King Grate?"

"Yes? What is it?" He looked back at his dormant grandmother. Sadness cast a dark shadow over his eyes.

Argan rode beside him and looked over her shoulder. She lowered her voice. "I know what vexes you."

"Many things do."

"Your grandmother will be safe with us. We will nurse her back to health."

"The healing strongwater is not working, and the Living Pools have shown no interest," he frowned.

"The elders will know what to do. We are family and we love you, Grate." She stared at him for a moment. "*I* love you."

"I love you too, Argan."

"Come again?"

"What?"

"What did you say?"

"Huh? I'm confused."

"You said Sara. You just called me Sara."

"What? I did not."

"You most certainly did."

"No, I didn't. Why would I say such a thing?" He cleared his throat and tried to remember what he'd actually said.

"Grate… is it true?"

"Is what true?"

Argan slowed her sea swallow and looked toward the sky again. "I will ride ahead. To make sure it is clear. Home is close." She made a clicking sound with her mouth to command her animal and quickly rode away.

The synthetic moon was full and bright. *Grandmother loves the round moon,* Grate thought.

Once they were back in the caves, Grate had a magnificent bed prepared for his grandmother next to his own. Lit flare-bark provided light throughout the chambers and created hypnotizing shadows all about. As Grate soaked his feet in pink strongwater, he realized that he hadn't seen Argan since they'd returned home. This was unusual. He was searching throughout the caves to find her when the smell of paint caught his attention. At last, he found her in one of the less-frequented cave cabins, painting a mural on the wall.

"Ahh, here you are." He crossed his arms and admired her work. "Is that Trepor and you?"

"It is."

"And the Breathing Valley!"

"Yep."

"I'm really impressed. The detail you gave to his skin is... wow! I miss him. I really do."

"As do I. He was my favorite brother."

"He was the best. He always knew what to say to lift my spirit. And I could never stay serious for long when he was around. Such a jokester!"

"Yep."

"Is something else the matter?"

Argan glanced at the king, then continued to paint.

"Argan, is something bothering you?"

"Yes."

"Well, will you tell me what's going on?" he laughed.

"No."

"Argan." Grate approached the small Surge and removed the painting instrument from her hand. "Talk to me. I beg of you."

His illuminous smile made her smile. She wished that it wasn't so easy for him to get a reaction from her. A shallow pool of glittery turquoise water next to them splashed at their feet. This particular pool enjoyed trailing Grate through the caves.

"My King, what do you think of me?"

"Excuse me?" he teased as he touched her forehead. "Are you feeling alright?"

"Please. What do you think of me?"

Grate sighed then dipped the paintbrush into Argan's yellow clay mixture and traced a figure on the wall. Argan frowned and began to tap her foot.

"Okay, Okay… I will leave your artwork as is."

"Please answer my question."

"Uhh, I think that you are brave and loyal. You are authentic and true."

"And?"

"And… irreplaceable. It's late. We should rest now."

"Do you find me beautiful?"

"Huh?"

"When you look upon me, is it beauty that you see?"

"All living beings possess a form of beauty."

"Grate…"

"What do you want from me? What's going on with you?"

"I need to know. Please?"

He placed the paintbrush on the floor and noticed that the pool of water had darkened to a red-wine color. It obviously didn't approve of the route in which the conversation was going. Grate shook his head and ignored it.

"I… do not see you in that way. We're friends. Best friends. But—"

"Well. Of course not. You are right. It is very late. May we win battles, even in our sleep." And as before, she abruptly left his side.

The pool, now deep blue and icy cold, threw itself against Grate's legs, then followed behind Argan.

"Oh, you as well?" Grate said to it. His voice echoed through the chamber. He took a seat and sat there for an hour in confusion. He'd never felt so lost and alone.

Later that night, King Grate tossed and turned in his sleep. The stones that were brought from Godmother's den began to gleam and emit energy throughout the chamber.

5-year-old Grate hears his praying grandmother before seeing her. I open then bats my eyes. Grandmother sits at my feet, beaming with gratitude.

    "I want my mommy," I say.

    "I know, dear. I know." She thanks God and wraps me in her arms and rocks me.

Grate moaned in his sleep.

Grandmother and I explore The Stretch. I am afraid at first. Godmother's long, wavy hair grows longer and longer, until it has passed her feet and surrounds the both of us. Down we slide, along her long, twisting mane. Then, I'm not afraid anymore! We study Bethiter's plants and animals. And what's that?!

    "A giant lizard!" I scream.

    "My name is Argan, you shell-less clam!"

Argan introduces us to her tribe. "I found shell-less clams! They are peaceful creatures... solely air breathers... weak, and ignorant. Let's help them!"

Argan grabs me by the hand and we dive into a pool of bright pink water. "This is the water of restoration! But never touch that over there... ooh, this clear berry is safe to eat and cures belly aches... remember the strongwater only heals wounds...and always respect the Living Pools..."

I grow taller as the old lady shrinks. My voice deepens. My jawline hardens. I grow hair everywhere. My Grandmother whispers, "You are a king! You have no choice but to be, Grate..."

    "I shall be your first kiss." I say to Argan.

    "Ew, get away!" We laugh and frolic then fall into nest of fire fairies.

    "Ouch! Ow! Grandmother, help us!"

"Grate, who do you fear?" Argan asks.
"Ha! I fear no one."
"I fear the one your kind call, Robot."
"Argan, I will protect you."

Dr. Robot appears; standing 20 feet tall with legs made of steel and his eyes are two hollow glass spheres. Then he starts to multiply. Hundreds of miniature metal-men sprout from him. They set fire to forests, seal caves shut, and rape and kill Surges.

"He took my mother! Mommy... I need you!"
"He took my mother too, Argan."
"He killed my father..."
"My father is dead to me too."

Twenty-five-year-old Grate stands before a large crowd. "Revolution!" I shout in an auditorium full of humans and Surges, but the people are turning into stone. One by one. I run up to each person but am unable to keep them from hardening.

Grate cried out in his sleep.

"Hear me, please!" My strong locs of hair turn gray and begin to grow. Longer and longer they spiral and overtake the theater. Then, I begin to rapidly increase in size. The Surges grab hold of my large ropes of hair and dangle as if cherries in a tree. Now a giant, I look down and see Dr. Robot and his gang. They are all very small.

"We are here. We will fight," Argan whispers into my giant ear.

Weeping is heard.

"Grandmother? Grandmother! Where are you?" Finally, I find her. Crying in her den. I don't know what to do. I stand there, with tiny Surges hanging from my hair.

"Grate. You must flee. You can no longer stay here," she laments.

"No!"

"Robot will kill you if he finds you."

"Come with us! Stay with us! Live with us!" The mini-Surges exclaim.

"Our world needs a king; yet, is not ready for one."

"Come with us! Be our king! Stay with us! Be our king! Live with us..."

I, the king, meet my grandmother in the Forbidden Valley.

"Come with me to the caves, Grandmother. You are too good for The Community."

"They need me as I need you. Never let your heart turn cold. Your soul cannot thrive with a cold heart. Believe... Life is More!"

I, the king, meet my grandmother in the Forbidden Valley.

I and my warriors prepare for war and meet her in the valley for ten years.

"Son, I am not alone this time. Someone needs my help." Out of the Godmother's long, thick, gray hair emerges a warm, bright light. The light consumes the pink valley strongwater and shines on me. I feel at home. Then we drink it together and dance. I walk into the light.

"Stay with me," I tell her.

"You know I can't. They'd come looking for me."

"Your light is the after-taste of heaven. I would give my all for you."

"I love you too much to let you do that."

"Don't forget me."

"To forget you would be impossible. I will love you forever, Grate."

"I will love you far longer than that... Until infinity runs out."

Flashes of colorful, wet light floods the valley. Red, blue, green, brown, orange, pink, black, violet, white, red... gray.

I spread the long, gray tresses like a curtain and hop out. I find myself in Godmother's den again. Her walking stick is leaning against the wall. Grandmother sits in her rocking chair, with her back to me.

 "I've found you! I've missed you."
 "Time is more precious than one can imagine, Grate. You must capture the essence of the Living Pools."
 "Capture them!? How will I ever do that?"
 "And save her."
 "Save who?"

 "Believe... Life is More!" Godmother starts to cry.

 "Don't fret, I will save her. Please, don't cry!"

An infant's cry can be heard along with Grandmother's. I cover my ears and plead for them to stop, only for the noise to intensify. I search the den with my eyes but see that I am now alone. The rocking chair is empty, and the walking stick is gone. Yet, the wailing continues. I fall to my knees then separate the back of my hair to reveal another, smaller ball of light. The most excellent light I've ever known.

 Then, it transforms into a newborn baby.

I hold her in my arms and she clings to me. Then the cries are heard no more.

Chapter Fourteen: The Weight of Words

The Parlimont household was also having an interesting night. Hampton had retired to his office and continued to drink once he returned home. His father had given him a collection of old journals, which included the past thirty years of his findings and experiments. Hampton gazed at the stack of books and leaned back in his chair. An old box of cigars also sat in front of him. He couldn't remember if they'd been gifted for the birth day of Hampton Nicholas or Brooks. He wondered who his sons would've grown to be. How they'd look. Maybe they would've had his green eyes or Sara's auburn hair? Could they have been musically inclined like his mother?

Or wicked... like his father?

Hampton took another shot of whiskey. He was determined to be a great father and all the things that *his* father wasn't... kind, patient, loving, *present*. It was Steddy who had taught him how to tie a tie and ride a bike. Hampton smiled at the thought of him running to his aid when he would fall off and scrape his knee.

Then he replayed how terrible his father had treated Steddy earlier that night and became infuriated. He eyed the journals once more.

"Aaaaaaarrgghhhhh!!!" he roared as he threw his whiskey glass across the room and shoved everything off his desk. He crashed back into his chair and began to sob.

Hardly thirty seconds later, there was a knock at the door. When Hampton didn't respond, the knocking continued.

"Everything's okay, James! No worries!" he called out as he laid his head on his desk.

"James isn't here! It's Garla. May I come in?"

Hampton didn't move.

"Hello? Hamp? Can you hear me?"

Hampton slowly lifted his head and opened his eyes to a spinning room. "What do you want?"

"May I please come in?"

"Go away! Ugh…"

"It's important. May I come in for just a minute?" she asked again.

"Oh, whatever… sure. Yes. Come in," he belched.

The large mahogany door opened and in walked Garla Lastoré. She'd changed out of her uniform and into a scantily clad nightgown.

"What a mess!" She looked around the room in shock.

"Yeah. So what?"

Garla slowly bent over to pick up the broken glass. And Hampton watched. She grinned.

"And these look valuable," she said as she returned the journals to the desk and took a seat beside them.

"What are you doing?" He squinted. "Where is your robe?"

"I thought you would like to know that Margot left work early."

"Maybe she's ill."

"No. She's up to something. I'm sure of it!"

"Garla, go to bed. You're so annoying sometimes." Hampton titled his head back and closed his eyes.

Garla hopped down from the desk and stood behind him.

"And *you* are so tense." She began to rub his neck. "And trusting. *Too* trusting."

Hampton hiccupped. "I wish you'd just go away."

"Oh, do you honestly mean that?" she purred and ran her fingers through his blonde hair. "I think that old man Steddy and Serenity are up to something, too. They might even be sleeping together."

"What?! They would never!" Hampton shouted. He attempted to stand, but Garla pushed him down by the shoulders.

"Shhhhh! I'm serious. You know I avoid trouble and keep to myself. I'm only telling you because I would hate to see you hurt, Hampster," she cooed as she massaged his neck and shoulders.

"Ah, no one's called me that since I was a kid," he chuckled.

"Listen, I caught Steddy leaving the nursery once Margot left. I heard some fuss about the baby or something."

"The baby?" He swiveled in his chair, so that he could face her.

"And when he left, he looked distraught..."

"What do you mean?"

"...As if he'd seen a ghost. *Or* been told that his secret love affair with his boss's wife produced a child."

Hampton thought for a moment. "Wait. No. No! You're insane! Get out of here, Garla! Go!" He stood and pointed toward the door.

"Think about it, Hampton!" She took a step closer. "All of the whispering and sneaking. The bizarre tension in the home. And the arguments. At least admit that the new baby looks different from the others."

"Fine, *I'll* go if you won't," Hampton turned to leave.

"Wait! Not to mention, Lucille was listening to your conversation with your father!" Garla gasped and covered her chest with her hands. She hadn't meant to tell the last part. "Oh, no..."

"What did you say?"

"I-I-I... I'm so sorry. Please don't hurt the girl!"

"You're right. It's time for me to put my foot down around here. They think they're going to disrespect me? ...in my own home?!" A large vein appeared between his eyebrows. His eyes bulged with fury.

Garla cowered. "Please, Hamp—"

"I'll show him! I'll show all of them," he shouted and slammed his hand on his father's journals.

What in Eternity's name have I done?! She thought.

The following morning was sunny, clear, and bright. The croaking and chirping of animals could be heard throughout The Community. Children merrily scattered and hid as "It" counted to ten underneath a tree. A group of toddlers waddled in the mud while their caregiver supervised. Some of the members bartered goods while others caught up on Bethiter gossip.

Margot sat up in her bed and yawned. Her face felt itchy and tight. "Oh, no!" she gasped as she touched her cheek and ran toward the mirror. She wet herself at the sight of her mutilated face and snow-white hair. Quickly, she ran to her washbowl to clean the dried blood and bits of flesh from underneath her fingernails. "Yea though

I walk through the valley of the shadow of death, I will fear no evil…" She scrubbed until her hands turned red.

An automobile's horn blared outside. Margot's heart thudded against her chest and she became paralyzed with fear.

"We are looking for Margot Stone!" a man's voice rang out. "Margot! If you can hear us, come outside!"

Margot scurried to her window to discover two of Dr. Parlimont's guards, from the previous night, standing in the yard. Members of The Community stared at the ground as they hurried away from the duo.

"How do we know that she's even here?" the younger guard whispered to the other.

"Where else would she be, Philip? … MARGOT STONE!" he continued.

"Who knows?" Philip eyed a group of young maids as they walked by. "Doc never mentioned that their women looked like *this!* My, my!"

"Hey, stay focused. I hear they're all diseased. And dirty."

"Yeah… *dirty!*" he grinned as he nudged his partner with his elbow.

"Quit playing around!" He cleared his throat and examined the exterior of the cabins as Margot watched in horror.

"Alright! Margot, I know you can hear me! We just want to talk. Come on out so we don't have to find you!"

They stared at the cabins and waited.

"It would be smart for you to come out, *NOW!*" the guard hollered. He then turned to his distracted partner. "Looks like we have to go in and search."

"Wait… Russ, look!"

For whatever reason, Margot opened her front door, left her porch, and stepped out onto the yard.

"Would you look at that…" Philip said with a confused expression.

Neither of them knew what to do. The front of Margot's gown was stained with breastmilk and her feet dripped with blood and urine. Her curly white hair sat all over her head, and her face was streaked with hideous, crusting wounds.

"I told you they were dirty," Russ whispered.

"I am Margot Stone," she calmly said.

After a moment, Russ cleared his throat. "The Parlimonts would like to meet your twins."

"What? But why?"

"We are to bring the three of you back to the manor. Come now."

"They're not here," a twisted grin grew across her lips.

"Stop with the madness! Come!" Russ lunged toward Margot and grabbed her by the arms while Philip ran into her cabin.

"No! No!" she screeched. "Come out of there! You have no right! Let me go! Why are you doing this?! Someone save me! Please!" she cried.

Members of The Community had assembled and helplessly watched as the two struggled. A nearby puddle turned clear and retracted beneath a cabin. Margot spat in the guard's face and pulled away with all her might.

"Uppity cosmic dust! I know what you need," he said as he yanked her closer. "Just wait until I get these cuffs on you and the two of us are in the back of the van."

"No!!!!" She tried to kick him in the groin but missed.

"There's no one here!" yelled Philip from the cabin. "She was right! We should go!"

"Where are they?!" Russ growled between clenched teeth. "Want to play rough?" He then grabbed Margot by the collar and punched her in the nose.

Her head flew back, and she slammed onto the ground.

"Whew! Man is she strong!" he chuckled. "I like that."

Philip shook his head in disappointment and exited the cabin. "Come on, we should head back." He stared at the ground as he advanced to the van.

"Not without those little sea monkeys! We were given an assignment, and—Aaargphhh!" Russ looked down to see a butcher knife wedged in his thigh.

An indignant and panting Margot stared at him as dark blood poured from her nose.

"What have you done?!" he muttered in disbelief. Drool fell from his trembling lips.

"Hey, Russ. Be cool. Russ! No!" Philip waved his arms in the air as he ran toward them.

Without hesitation, the injured guard retrieved his pistol from his side and shot Margot in the top of her head. And for the first time ever, The Community went silent.

"Help me to the van, will you?" Russ said.

Chapter Fifteen: Lucille Too

Lucille jumped up from her bed of soft leaves and looked around. Her brothers were peacefully sleeping next to her. A flock of birds flew overhead.

"What was that?" she said to herself. She'd made a decent shelter using branches and their extra clothes. It was comfortable and safe. She wondered if it was truly necessary to journey deeper into The Stretch. But then she considered how adamant her mother was about them reaching The Breathing Valley.

One of her brothers began to stir. Lucille smiled. After feeding and changing the twins, Lucille broke down their little hut and proceeded to follow the trail that the map outlined. The "sun" was particularly bright that morning, which made carrying the boys and her full satchel daunting.

Suddenly, a peculiar feeling came over her. She checked her surroundings but saw no one. Though she continued to march forward, she was certain that someone… or something was following her. She began to speed up her pace. Sounds of breaking twigs echoed behind her. Then, she began to run. Steps could now be heard advancing near her. Lucille shrieked and took off running at full speed. Forgetting the route, she made an abrupt turn that led uphill. Faster and faster she ran until her legs began to burn. Knowing that she couldn't go on for much longer, she peeked over her shoulder but sadly, tripped over a log in the process. Unable to keep her balance with the extra weight that she carried, the young girl fell over to her right. Her ankle snapped, and she howled out in pain and tumbled down the hillside. As she descended, thorny vines mocked her and tugged at her hair and clothes, grumpy rock creatures dug into her sides, and umpteen items flew out of her bag. By the time she reached the base of the high ground, poor Lucille was left unconscious and one of her brothers had a cracked skull.

"Change into another apron, Lucille. I see a spot on that one," Margot suggested as she rested in bed. "The Parlimonts are decent people. Mister Parlimont keeps to himself and spends most of his time down in the lounge or upstairs in his study. Missus

Parlimont is due any day now and on her fourth try. As you can imagine she spends much of her day in bed."

Lucille nodded and tied the new apron around her waist. "Plus, Uncle Steddy is always there!" she said with a smile. She paused, then turned to her mother. "How come he never comes home?"

"That's grownup business. And you are not a grownup."

"Can I ask him?"

"No. Plus it's '*May* I ask…'."

Lucille rolled her eyes then admired her reflection in a mirror. "I have a job!"

"Ehh, not my choice. Your brothers arrived sooner than expected and Missus Parlimont needs companionship. Oh, and remember to stay clear of the other maid, Garla. She's an evil Surge in human skin!"

On her third day working at the manor, Lucille was assigned to clean the Parlimont's bedroom and purge everything related to the most recent baby. While doing so, she came across Mrs. Parlimont's diary. Being the inquisitive pre-teen that she was, Lucille hid the notebook under her apron and headed for the secret hideout space in the linen room. Reading the diary became sort of pastime for her.

February 12, 19

Today, the doctor confirmed that I'm pregnant. Hamp and I are elated and hopeful. I have been adhering to the doctor's orders for the past two years. The dreadful prenatal regimen has been grueling: the injections, the vitamins, the tests. But in the end, we will have a healthy baby, who will live and prosper. It's too early to determine the sex, but I have a feeling that it will be a girl!

November 23, 20

It has taken me this long to acknowledge the loss of Tre. I miss him every day.

And I'm with pregnant again. My intention was to wait a little longer before doing this again. I visit the doctor three times a week and he's advised that I only get out of bed if necessary. Hampton has hired the very best physicians to look after me. I've been spotting for a week and fear that this is a terrible omen; but, the doctor says that it's normal. My morning sickness has caused me to lose weight. My hallowed cheeks make me look like a skeleton. I often wonder if Hamp still finds me beautiful. Although I am trying to enjoy my pregnancy, it's extremely difficult to do so.

December 4, 21

I lost the baby last night. Nick blames it on my spicy food cravings and uncommon food combinations, although I'm certain that's not the reason.

October 28, 22

We welcomed Hampton Nicholas over the weekend. He arrived a couple days early, and of course we didn't mind at all. He is a beautiful and healthy baby boy. He sleeps during the day and likes to be entertained at night, just as he was in the womb. One of the hospital's most experienced nurses has moved in and she's been wonderful. She was a nurse in the Old World and tells me about how things used to be. No one has determined why the babies keep passing away; but, she's sure that the doctors and scientists will have a cure soon. In the meantime, we're taking all precautions and steps to give him the chance at life. Naturally, I'm afraid. But if I lose hope, what will I have left?

August 17, 23

Sweet Hampton Brooks' ceremony is in the morning. His eyes turned from gray to blue on his final day. And he had the cutest dimple in his chin. He made it to seven days and we were so sure that this time would be different. Hamp won't even look at me. I'm ashamed and feel that this is my fault. I'm tired in every way possible. He has his golfing buddies, his studies, and his whiskey. But what do I have? The other wives refuse to discuss the matter, even though it has happened to us all. A sinful recurrence. Am I to suffer alone for eternity? I don't see how that is fair.

September 1, 23

I caught Garla sneaking into Hamp's office last night. She mocks me with her stares and patronizing questions. I want her to leave my house. But, in all honesty, this is as much her home as it is mine. And as for Hampton, I guess my only option is to share him as well. He sleeps in one of the guest bedrooms now. We share no intimacy or passion. When he comes to my bedroom, it's merely a routine. His only mission is to impregnate me. We don't speak to each other. We don't eat together. He didn't even acknowledge my birthday today. Mr. Watters gave me a card and made a delicious sponge cake. Honestly, I'm repulsed by Hamp's smell now. I feel trapped in my own home and skin. When we go into town, we put on a great show. I wonder if other marriages suffer in silence too. It's an exhausting existence.

September 3, 23

Every morning I wake up, I cry and curse at the stars. I don't want to live any longer. I feel as though a moon sits on my shoulders. I don't want to eat or bathe or breathe. I used to be so beautiful. What's the point of any of this? I was told Mother took her life by slitting her wrists... but I'd never be that brave. I plan to disguise myself and somehow sneak to The Community late tonight. I hear that there's an old woman there, they call her "Godmother," who has all sorts of potions and remedies made from Bethiter's natural resources. I need a remedy to life. I can't take another day.

September 7, 23

I'm happy to write that I'm still alive. I traveled to The Community and the most glorious thing occurred. The Godmother refused to sell me any toxic greens and instead, told me that I have a purpose. She spoke life into my empty vessel. She encouraged me and rocked me like a newborn baby as I cried in her lap. We went to a secret place and I drank this mysterious pink water from the valley. I was so afraid. But I trusted her, more than I've ever trusted anyone. And, I met a man. I don't have the words to describe my encounter. I wish to go back. In fact, I didn't want to leave. However, she says that I'm cured and that I'm to never return. All of the money in Bethiter isn't enough to repay her.

September 22, 23

I'm pregnant again and there's something very different about this time. I haven't experienced any nausea or heartburn and have the energy of a teenaged girl. I haven't told Hamp. I don't feel that he's worthy of this gift. Is that selfish of me? I reject him now when he comes to my bedroom. I deserve more than to be treated as wild stock. The baby moves a lot whenever I'm near water. It's the most peculiar thing. And there's something else. Ever since my time in the valley, Grate, the man from the caves, permeates my dreams. I long for him the way the flowers long for the sun. Every day I consider returning to The Stretch alone to see him once again. I will go back to be with Grate when I get the opportunity. Me and my baby. Perhaps I'm going insane.

Refreshing rose-colored water turned Lucille onto her side and pounced across her battered face. Some of it dove into her nose, ears, and mouth as well. Other streams of the water gently massaged her legs. Upon reaching the baby boys, the flowing water transformed into a thick, pink vapor and quickly entered their noses. The twins started to squirm. Lucille's body went stiff and began to violently convulse. She tried to cry out for her mother but couldn't. After what felt like ages, Lucille's body finally relaxed.

"Thank… you…" she whispered.

The vapor returned to its liquid state and then ran away. Lucille sat up and quickly unwrapped the sling to check her brothers. They were unharmed and well. Then she noticed that she wasn't wearing her bag anymore. And the map was nowhere to be found. Lucille frantically looked around, for the map, a pouch of milk, or even an extra sweater, but to no avail.

"We're going to die," she said as she sat on the ground.

"Who is going to die?" asked a voice.

"Who's there?! Hello?!" Lucille yelled. She scooped up her brothers and grabbed the wrap and looked all around.

"I am here," said the voice. "I am the tree."

Sweat appeared across Lucille's forehead and her legs became weak. She was standing in the middle of countless trees and wondered why anyone would play such a cruel joke at a time like this.

After a moment, one of the trees started to shake, then morphed into another Lucille!

"Now I am you." It waved and smiled.

"Whoah…" whispered Lucille.

"Who are you?" the second Lucille asked.

"*I* should be asking *you* that!" Lucille nervously responded.

"Why?"

"Well, because… because you're me," Lucille answered while she quickly placed her brothers back into the halter.

"How do you know that you are not me?"

"Are you kidding me right now?" Lucille shook her head and looked up toward the sky. She wondered what time it was.

"It is after noon." The second Lucille reported.

"Thanks." Lucille gave a skeptical look. "Can I ask a question?"

"You can do whatever suits you."

"*May* I ask a question?"

"Yes. However, I may not answer."

"Why not?"

"Because I may not have the desire." The second Lucille gave a friendly smile and began to skip away.

"Hold on, wait!" Lucy trotted behind her clone. "Where are you going?"

"I do not know. Where are you going?"

"Well, I was intending on reaching the Breathing Valley, but I've lost my map. And my food. And my clothes."

"You are wearing clothes."

"I mean my extra clothes."

"I hope that you find them," the second Lucille sincerely offered.

"Thank you."

"Where is your mate?"

"My mate? I don't have a mate. I'm too young!"

The second Lucille stopped walking at stared at Lucille. "Then how do you explain those?"

"Oh, these are my brothers! My siblings."

"Where is your mother?"

"That is a very complicated story."

The second Lucille blinked and continued to stare.

"…A very complicated story that I'd rather not discuss," Lucille continued. "So, what are you?"

"I am me."

"No, *what* are you?"

"I am here."

"Listen to me carefully, I am a human girl. What are you?"

"Why does that matter?

"Well, I suppose it doesn't," shrugged Lucille.

"It does not. I am whatever I desire to be." The second Lucille blinked and started skipping again.

Lucille scratched her head in confusion as she followed. "How do you usually look?"

"However I like."

"Okay…" Lucille chuckled. "How would you look if you hadn't met me?"

"I do not know."

"Well, do you have a name? Mine is Lucille."

"I will be Lucille, too then."

"Alright, I will call you Lucille Two."

"Alright."

"Where is your home, Lucille Two?"

"You are odd."

"Excuse me?"

"You say that you are without food, adequate clothing, and the map, yet you only speak of me. Those fry will need shelter. They will need a home."

"We have a home. Well, we did. But, I had to flee The Community to protect my brothers. I fell down this huge hill and nearly died… But then a mystifying water revived me!"

"That was the Living Pool. It protects infants, seniors, and imbeciles."

"But I'm not an infant or a senior," Lucille rebutted.

Lucille Two nodded.

As they walked, Lucille began to explain how she'd found herself deserted in The Stretch— from the Parlimonts and Dr. Robot, to the Surges and King Grate.

"I know the king."

"You do?? He's my mother's cousin. I wish you would've told me!"

"You did not ask."

"Would you mind taking me there? To the king?"

"No."

"No? But—"

"I would not mind." Lucille Two paused briefly; and then turned left. "This way."

After about two hours of walking… and Lucille talking, Lucille Two abruptly stopped.

"The Great King and his soldiers reside over there. Between the Forbidden Valley and Fire Fairy Forest."

"Oh, thank Eternity!" an exhausted Lucille proclaimed. "My brothers are hungry. But… why have you stopped walking?"

"I am bored. I wish to travel in a different direction."

"Wait, but I need you, Lucille Two."

"You do not need me, Lucille the human girl. Goodbye." The duplicate Lucille waved and smiled once more; then merrily skipped away.

Chapter Sixteen: The Fire Fairy Forest

Earlier the same morning, Grate called Argan into his chamber to devise a plan to carry out the mission from his dream. The Godmother tranquilly slept on her ornate bed. It was decorated with colorful flowers and fragrant herbs. One of the elder Surges brushed her long, gray hair and applied valley oil to her scalp.

"Grandmother looks as if she's smiling," said Grate as he respectfully stood and motioned for Argan to take a seat across from him at his table.

"Indeed, she does. Did you sleep well?"

"No. Did you?"

"No. I dreamed that I lost Trepor over and over again. It haunts me while I sleep and more so when I am awake. I miss my brother so much, I feel I may go mad."

"I know. And I am sorry. It pains me to see you suffering. If I could give you peace, I would."

"I know."

Grate held his head back as he tied his long locs of hair with a leather-bark band. He exhaled then leaned forward to his devoted friend. He didn't want the Surge, who was pampering his grandmother, to overhear him. "Argan, I have a plan. Do not panic, alright?"

"Of course, I will not panic. Go on."

He studied her with intense discernment. "Listen, we must find a way to contain some of the Living Pools," he whispered.

"What?!" Flabbergasted, Argan jumped to her feet and began to pace back and forth.

"Shhhh! Calm down! Hear me out—"

"This is absurd, Grate. Do you realize that it has never been done? The Living Pools are to be feared and left alone!"

"I know."

"They are the oldest creatures in existence. They travel and commit as they please."

"I know. I know."

"You are my leader. You are my king. At your command, I would travel to the ends of Mother Infinity. I would risk my life a thousand times over for you. Normally, whatever you order, I follow without question. But this time—"

"Then why start questioning now?" Grate stood and gently placed his large hands on Argan's shoulders. "If you'll trust me, then trust me with all of your heart. If you'll go with me, then go all the way... with all of your might. I believe that we'll be victorious. There's no other way."

Argan shook her head. "How will we ever capture the essence of the Living Pools? How can it be done?"

"Just know that even if we can't... we will."

After packing food and other necessities, Grate and Argan rode their noble sea swallows through the hilly Stretch. Oodles of small geysers erupted around them as they headed toward the Fire Fairy Forest. It was said that fire fairies were direct decedents of stars and arguably just as old, if not older, than the Living Pools. The only problem was that the tiny bodies of light weren't exactly congenial. But Grate hoped to meet with the Fire Fairy Queen and possibly gain insight on how to persuade the Living Pools to join them.

The two were riding in silence, each nervous about their upcoming encounter with the fairies, when a flock of squawking birds flew overhead.

"They're from The Community," Great observed.

"Something must be wrong," added Argan.

Grate stopped his sea swallow and cased their surroundings. "We are too much in the sun. Let's go this way. It'll take longer, but we will be safe."

Hours of traveling through a wooded area passed, and the pair became weary. Argan asked for a break and quickly dismounted her ride to excuse herself behind a tree. Grate used the time to walk around and stretch his back. He poured cool water down his sweaty chest, then retired next to a large, moss-covered rock as scenes from the previous night's dream replayed in his mind.

"How are you, my king?" Argan asked. She rubbed her backside with both hands and gave a bashful smile. "We have been riding for a long time."

"Yes, I'm paying for it too," Grate agreed as he tossed the canteen of water her way. "Come rest with me." He reclined on the ground and surveyed the sky. "When I was a boy, my grandmother would tell me tales that her grandmother learned from *her* grandmother, about how our people could fly long, long ago."

"Fly?!" she laughed. "But your kind can barely swim!"

"Hey! Watch yourself." Grate threw moss at Argan and continued. "After being captured from their lands, my people forgot their worth. They forgot all of the light that they possessed. Their minds became confined and they could no longer fly."

"Oh."

"That is precisely what has happened here."

"I see."

"My family worked hard on the Old World and sacrificed their all to come here. If only I could remind them of their power! How do I make them understand that they deserve more than what they accept?"

"I do not know. But I am certain that you can find a way."

"Yeah. I want better for us. For all of us. There's so much more in life just waiting to be savored."

Argan admired the king. Her green eyes began to lighten.

"What's on your mind, Argan?"

"Huh? Oh." She looked away from him. "Grate, I was wondering… do you suppose that there is any truth to the Robot's assumption? About the hearts of your community being stronger than others?"

"I'm not certain. Even though…" he stopped.

"What is it?"

He gathered his thoughts, then began to explain. "Long before I was born, my community was used for experiments in the Old World, too."

"Experiments? On your old planet?"

"Yes. It's thought, by some, that the trauma and stress passed genetically."

"What? I do not understand."

He sighed. "Grandmother would say that the trauma was in our blood. That the grief and anger from thousands of years ago was passed down from one generation to the next. The pain of being torn from their homes... enslaved... treated worse than animals... was all passed down. With each new generation came a new strength. She said we were born to survive anything," he shrugged and fidgeted with the moss in his hands. "She used to say that all of the suffering gave us "durable hearts and an extra soul." It was necessary for survival... from the Motherland to Bethiter."

"The Motherland... I like that." She yawned and looked up toward the sphere and thought of Mother Infinity. "Grate?"

"Yes?"

She turned to look at him. "Do you think that Robot experimented on Trepor?"

"Don't think about that. I hate to think of what he is capable of doing. He thrives from the sorrow that he inflicts on others. So, instead, I want you to think of all of the happy times you shared with your brother."

Argan took a deep breath and blinked away her tears. "Like the time he fell in love with a mermaid and tried to make a potion, so he could trade his legs for a fish's tail?!"

They both laughed.

"Yes. Think of him that way."

"I will. Thank you."

"It is my pleasure to make you smile, Argan."

Her eyes twinkled once more.

"Very well then," Grate said as he rose to his feet, oblivious to her golden eyes. "The fire fairies aren't too far from here. We should get going." He reached for Argan's hand to help her up.

"I have never seen anyone excited about being stung to death."

"Hey, life's no fun without a little danger!" He tickled her sides and ran behind a tree to dodge her.

She chased him until he reached his sea swallow.

"You'll never catch me!" he teased.

"I have realized," she said to herself.

Half an hour or so later, the two reached the Fire Fairy Forest. They waited and stared at tall, brawny trees. The branches shot from the upper portion of the trunks and their flat, waxy leaves were dark green and various sizes.

"Shall we?" Grate hopped to the ground. He began putting on thick leather-bark sleeves and leggings. Argan did the same.

"Are you ready?" he asked.

Together they entered the forest. And… nothing happened. After walking around for a while, the Surge and king presumed it safe to relax. The shade from the trees was pacifying and the forest was proving to be more pleasant than they'd anticipated.

"It's beautiful here, Argan. We should explore the planet more."

"After you have seen one forest, you have essentially seen them all," Argan shrugged. "Ooh, water-berry vines! I cannot remember the last time I tasted these. Here, you must try!" She plucked some berries from their fuzzy vines and popped them into the king's mouth.

"Mmmmm! These *are* good! Could we grow some in the caves?"

"Probably not. The caves are too dark," she said between chews. "One time," she snickered. "Trepor ate so many of these that his mouth was blue for a week!"

"A week?!"

They continued to share endearing stories about Trepor as they strolled through the romantic woods.

A faint twinkle in the distance gradually approached the couple.

"How fascinating!" whispered Argan as she tucked a handful of water-berry vines into one of her pockets.

It was a single, yellow fire fairy. It curiously hovered in place before coming face- to-face with them. Grate held out his hand and moved closer to it. Suddenly, the fiary began to flash its light from yellow to red as it became brighter and warmer. Next, out of nowhere thousands of fire fairies swarmed from the trees and began to strike the intruders. There were so many that the various shades of red, yellow, orange, white, and green appeared as a bright, magnificent blur.

"No! Stop, please! We come in peace! We come in peace!!" Grate dropped to his knees with his arms lifted to the sky.

"I cannot see! Yiiiipe!" Argan screeched. "They are burning me all over!"

The two began to roll and toss their bodies across the ground; but that didn't stop the fairy attack. The pain was crippling. And as if the burns from their rays weren't excruciating enough, the fire fairies ridiculed the pair all the while.

"You should not have come here!"

"How dare you, air breather?!"

"Leave!"

"Disgusting creatures!"

"You are not welcome here!"

"Foolish cave-dwellers!"

"How does our light feel, you trespassers?!"

"Go! Go now!"

"Use your powers, Argan! Wave them off!" Grate cried as the fire fairies flew underneath his armor and clothing.

"I am trying! I am no match for them!"

"Grab on to me! We have to get out of here!"

After what seemed like forever, they finally found their way out of the forest. Grate's eyes were swollen shut. Argan staggered to his sea swallow and retrieved the pink valley strongwater from his bag and doused herself with it.

"Hold your head back, your Majesty." She allowed some of it to fall onto his eyes and spotted face.

Next, they removed their gear and tried to catch their breath. Lashes and burns covered their bodies but were instantly soothed after the healing water was applied.

"What in the sphere were we thinking?!"

"Exactly. That was a horrible idea," said Argan with her hands on her hips. She closed her eyes and thanked her ancestors for letting her make it out in one piece.

Unexpectedly, one of the nearby trees begins to wobble.

"Oh, no!" Grate complained as he and Argan lunged for cover.

Seconds later, they were relieved to see the tree transform into an Argan look-alike.

"Hello, King Grate. Hello, Argan." Lucille Two smiled and approached the edgy twosome.

"Oh, it's you, Jixt! We're so glad to see you," exclaimed Grate as he held his chest and sighed. "We thought you were another fairy."

"My name is not Jixt anymore. It is now Lucille Two."

"Well of course. Please forgive me."

"You are looking well, old friend," Argan smirked.

"Thank you. You are not," Lucille Two replied. She admired her new colorful skin then gave a look of disappointment once she realized that her rump had no tail.

"Ghrrrr…" growled Argan.

"The fire fairies do not like outsiders."

"We are aware," Argan said as she watched her replica spin around.

"Then you should not have entered."

"Hey! I have an idea, Jixt!" Argan approached her clone and stopped her from moving. "I mean, Lucille Two."

"Yes?"

"You could shift into a fairy and reach the queen for us!"

"I could."

"Would you mind? It is crucial that we speak with her."

"No."

"No?"

"I would not mind."

"Fantastic! Please inform whomever you speak with that we mean no harm and desperately need to see the Queen Fairy."

"You only *want* to see her."

"Right." Grate nodded. "We want to see the queen."

Lucille Two nodded with him then, all at once, transformed into an orange fire fairy. She circled Argan's head a couple of times before landing on her nose.

"Be nice," whispered the amused king. "Great idea by the way."

"I am going into the forest now," gave Lucille Two's squeaky fairy voice.

"Take your time," mumbled Argan.

Lucille Two fluttered off into the woods. Just then, a stream of Living Pools flowed up to them and waited. As much as it craved the fairies' potent energy, it would never dare to enter the forest. The heat from their light, all together, would evaporate the pool effortlessly.

"Hmm, Lucille… that name is familiar."

"It *is* familiar," Grate replied.

"Is it not the name of the young maiden from The Community, who wished to marry you?"

"Oh, her... no. I believe her name was Lizzie. She was assertive, that one."

"Was it the name of your grandmother's pet turtle from years back?"

"No. Her name was Lucinda or something like that."

"Lucinda! Right. She had a gorgeous shell."

"Indeed. Who in the sphere is Lucille?" Grate didn't want to dedicate any more time on the enigma. Instead, he made a funny face at Argan and made her laugh.

It didn't take long for Lucille Two to return from the forest. She flickered as she landed on Argan's nose again. Grate chuckled to himself.

"The queen will meet you. She says do not insult her with your useless armor. Goodbye!" Lucille Two kissed Argan's forehead then flew away.

The resting pool rippled as the fairy passed by and quickly followed her.

"Wait!" Argan yelled. "Who is Lucille? Jixt! Have you visited The Community?" But, it was too late and Lucille Two didn't turn back.

"Come on. Let's go," suggested Grate. "Should we bring this along?" He waved the small bottle of healing water in the air.

"Probably not. The less reason for them to attack, the better."

"I agree," he sighed.

Each of them performed a personal ritual of something close to thoughtful breathing, a prayer, and a moment of wondering what would happen if they packed up and simply went back home. They both knew that they were stalling. Neither cared.

"Here goes nothing," Argan managed to say with pep.

Grate took her by the hand and together they reentered the fire fairy's domain. As before, they saw nothing out of the ordinary at first. But suddenly, the entire forest illuminated with a multitude of fire fairies. It was surreal and bright, as if walking into a miniature galaxy. The two were so mesmerized by the sight that they didn't notice that a plump purple fairy had flown up to them.

"Greetings! I am Velorum X, Queen Omnia's assistant. Please follow me."

Velorum X led them deeper into the forest and up into one of the unusually large trees. It was sturdy enough that the two were able to walk along the branches with ease. They were seated where the branch met the tree trunk. And in the trunk was a large hollow space. The other thousands of fairies gathered around in the tree and stared at the guests. Most of them had never seen a human before.

"The air breathers are real?!" a young fairy whispered to her mother with merriment.

The royal trumpets sounded throughout the forest and everyone stood... or hovered as the Fire Fairy Queen arrived and found her place in the middle of the trunk's opening. Everyone bowed in her presence. She had a unique, spiraling light and was the only dark blue fairy there. A sheer train of sparkling dust fell from her as she waited for Velorum X to instruct that the audience be seated.

"Hello, you two. I am Queen Omnia Stella Astrum. Welcome to my forest," gave the queen.

"Your Majesty, thank you for seeing us. My name is Grate and this is my friend, Argan."

"I apologize for my nation's aggression earlier; although, you should know better than to enter without an invitation."

"Please forgive us."

"What brings you?"

"We are in need of your wisdom."

"Is that so?"

"Yes. We are under attack by the one called Doctor Robot. He has committed vicious and unspeakable crimes against the natives of this land as well as his own kind. He must be stopped."

"Is he responsible for this ghastly barrier between here and Mother Infinity?"

"He is."

The queen lowered her gaze with a look of uneasiness. It was uncommon for her to be speechless. The surrounding fairies began to twinkle and whisper amongst themselves in language that Grate couldn't understand.

"We have been imprisoned for decades. We have been cut off from our families and become hostages in our own home. I will gladly do all that is in my power to rid this place of the... ehm... 'Robot' and reunite my kingdom with the exterior pools. What do you request from me?"

"To face him," Grate swallowed. "We would like to obtain essence of the Living Pools."

Gasps were heard through the fairy audience. The queen's eyes widened from shock. She and Velorum X slowly turned to one another. He blinked. Then, the queen politely covered her mouth as she started to giggle. Next, Velorum X's shoulders began to bounce as he tried to contain his chuckling. But this caused the queen to erupt into uncontrollable laughter. The queen flashed from blue to white and continued to flicker as she doubled over with glee. Peals of laughter were heard throughout the forest. Grate lowered his head in shame. Argan crossed her arms and was reminded of all the negative things she'd heard about the crude fire fairies.

"Please pardon my laughter. You cannot be serious!" The queen wiped tears from her eyes.

"We should go." Grate had never been so humiliated.

"No! We have come too far." Argan unfolded her arms and stepped forward. "Your Majesty, we are as serious as a star attack."

The surrounding fairies began to quiet down.

"I am Argan'Basileum, of the Onyx Caves. My tribe has dwelled in the caves from the beginning of light and are faithful guardians of the core. We too have suffered endlessly due to the barrier between the terrain and Mother Infinity. The Robot has stolen our land. He has torn our families apart. He has created wounds that no waters will ever heal. I regret that we arrive under such circumstances; as we should have joined forces long before now. We humbly beseech you to be our ally so that we may defeat this earthly evil; for, anything less than resistance will surely result in our demise." A single tear ran down Argan's face.

The forest fell completely silent. A quieting air filled the space and discouraged any opposing energy. Grate's eyes welled with tears as thoughts of his mother, Trepor, his grandmother, and the baby consumed his mind. He was also proud and thankful to have Argan as a friend. His emotions exceeded anger and the desire for revenge. He merely wanted peace. And contentment. He wanted to live his life without fear of being murdered for being born.

Believe… Life is More!

"I concur," stated the queen. She took some time to think. "I will send Ria, my most vigorous warrior, to accompany you. She will not let you down." She introduced a light blue fairy, who floated to her side.

"It is a privilege to be at your service," Ria proclaimed with a bow.

Argan and Grate respectfully bowed their heads.

"With that being said," continued the queen, "In regard to the Living Pools, you must seek counsel from another."

"We are grateful, queen. May your flame continue to burn throughout Mother Infinity until light exists no more," Argan gave, still bowing.

Grate thought of the baby from his dream. "So, who should we contact—"

"Before anything else, let us bless the three of you and give thanks in advance for a triumphant quest!" said the queen.

Still in the trees, the two guests were guided to a wash area, where they cleaned themselves and prepared for dinner. Next, they sat at a long dining table made of coral, before a florid feast. Melodic chimes and hypnotic drums played in the background as everyone ate and became better acquainted. A parched Grate gulped his drink and placed his empty chalice onto the table.

"Now that is *really* tasty!" He wiped the corners of his mouth with his hand.

"Be careful, king," the queen warned with a smile. "Liquid light does not hit the belly immediately!"

"Aw, I can handle it! Fill me up!"

"Hear, hear!" shouted Velorum X as he raised his own chalice.

Everyone cheered and for the night, though transient, all was well in their world.

"Dance with me!" Grate grabbed Argan by the hand and ushered her to her feet. He held the small of her back and pulled her close to him with care.

"You have had too much to drink, my Lord!" She smiled with her eyes. Even after a full day of travel, the king smelled like cool water-mint to her. She breathed him in.

Queen Omnia and her court chatted amongst themselves as they looked on. Ria pointed toward the pair with one hand and made a gesture pointing to her head, suggesting that they were crazy, with the other. The gossiping group found it most bewitching to witness two very different species interacting in such a manner.

"We have been through so much together... My bold and daring Argan," Grate said as they danced. "You are more than beautiful. You are more than brave. There isn't a word for what you are. But I can feel it... here. And I need you." Still holding her hand, Grate pointed to his heart. He stared into her emerald eyes, which began to lighten to a golden-yellow.

She blushed and looked away. Grate smiled to himself and licked his lips. He pulled her even closer.

"Wait."

"But why?" Grate touched her chin to bring her face to his.

"No."

"No?"

"No, Grate!" Argan broke from her stupor; ashamed. She loosened her hold from around his neck and looked him square in the eyes. "Do you truly desire me? Are you bored? Or drunk? Or just naturally obtuse? Do not insult me with arbitrary banter or vapid attempts, Grate. I am to be loved and honored and valued. I am more than a distraction or afterthought. Make a choice!" she huffed and pushed him away from her before returning to her seat at the table.

Grate was stunned by it all and wondered if it was his breath that offended her. Before he could rejoin her, the royal trumpets sounded once more, and everyone began to rise. The entire party stared in reverence as The Queen Mother, a bright, black fairy arrived to the festivities. She moved slowly as her train of wiry, flashing gray lights shimmered behind her.

Grate tip toed to Argan and whispered in her ear. "I have never seen a black star! I cannot believe this! I wish Trepor—"

"Please be quiet and give me space," Argan quickly assumed a pleasant expression and stood tall, even though she noticed the onlookers, who'd witnessed the rift between the two.

"Honored guests, this is my mother, Queen Gloria Stella Astrum. It is a rare treat to have her join us tonight!"

The crowed whistled and cheered.

Grate belched. "Do you suppose that I could have more of the light?" he asked
Argan as he pointed to his chalice.

"Get it together, Grate! Focus!" she said behind her smile as she applauded with everyone else. "Excuse me, server… would you please pour some water for the king? Regular water. Yes. Thank you."

"You used to be fun," he sulked.

The Queen Mother cleared her throat. "Greetings in the name of Mother Infinity and everything that is true! I am very glad to be here. I am old and cannot be upright for long; but I wanted to meet the ones, who are on a mission to destroy the great barrier. Ria, my radiant kinsfairy, I trust that you will exemplify the light and only the light."

Ria bowed.

The Queen Mother caught her breath and studied Grate and Argan with intensity. "To the one that they call king, do not be preoccupied by what appears to be worthwhile. Open your mind to new knowledge and open your heart to forgiveness. I bless you in the name of all things pure and purposeful. Return to your source."

"To the guardian of the core, cherished treasure, who does not treasure herself: From this point onward, no longer wait to be granted permission to access things that already belong to you. No longer seek the approval of those who should be impressing you. The living water runs through your veins. You are a queen! You were born wearing a crown. I bless you in the name of all things pure and purposeful. May the forces of the Great Forever and

Mother Infinity guide and protect you both, not only during battle, but for the rest of your days!"

She then turned to the crowd, with her arms held high. "May our ancestors in Mother Infinity align to lead and cover us all!"

The forest roared with praise. Argan looked over at Grate, whose hands were covering his face. Tears escaped his palms and streamed down the insides of his wrists and forearms. She placed her hand on his back in support. The stars outside of the sphere shined brighter and rejoiced.

Chapter Seventeen: The Dejected Mountain

The next morning, Grate, Argan, and Ria left the Fire Fairy Forest to head for Mount Dejected, the tallest mountain on the planet. The queen had explained that this is where they could learn how to capture some of the Living Pools.

"If the pools will listen to anyone, it is the Moon Fish, at the Dejected Mountain. It will be challenging to reach him, and he is not fond of strangers," she'd said.

Grate was surprised by how rejuvenated he felt, even though he'd gotten very little sleep the night before. Argan felt renewed also and had slept peacefully and nightmare-free. Ria flew in between the two as they rode their sea swallows through the rugged region of The Stretch.

Grate turned to the captivating fairy. "It's a pleasure to have you with us, Ria. If you get tired of flying, feel free to hitch a ride."

"I appreciate that. And I thank you for having me. I am happy that we have finally met. There are no reasons why intelligent creatures cannot intermingle and get along."

"I agree," said Grate. He glanced at Argan, but she only looked ahead.

"And now, we fairies can come to the caves for the wedding!"

"Wedding? What wedding?" Argan's head jerked in Ria's direction.

"Are you not betrothed to King Grate?"

"No!" they both said in unison.

"Oh. My mistake. I apologize. This is quite awkward." Ria was amused by their reactions.

The three continued the journey in silence. Eventually, their destination could be seen in the distance.

"The Dejected Mountain!" Ria pointed.

"Thank goodness." Argan was eager to proceed to the next stage of the mission. She could feel Grate staring at her but refused to look at him. She grunted.

"What is the matter?" Ria began to fly backward so that she could face the peeved Surge.

"Nothing," said Argan.

"I did not mean to pry."

"It is alright."

"Are you sad?"

"No."

"Are you anxious?"

"No."

"Are you tired after last night's dancing?"

"No!"

Grate shook his head and knew that it was best to stay out of the conversation. Argan wasn't easy to talk to when she was angry.

Then Ria decided to focus on Grate and left Argan to fly beside him. "King, may I ask a question?"

As long as it has nothing to do with my love life or how I am feeling. "Sure. Ask away."

"Now, why are we battling the Robot?"

"Because he is detrimental to the planet."

"Perhaps I did not phrase my question correctly. Why now? He has been plaguing us for over eight cycles… twenty of your years I mean."

Grate thought for a moment. "He has plans to kill the young of my family."

Argan smirked.

"I see," Ria sighed.

"What is it?"

"Do I have permission to speak freely?"

"Yes," Argan said.

"King, do I have *your* permission?"

Argan rolled her eyes and took a deep breath.

"Of course. Speak freely, Ria," answered Grate.

"It is disheartening that you only chose to act when the threat became personal. Yet, you sought outsiders for help."

Argan glared at the her.

"We have been hiding in the forest all of this time in fear. We have been segregated from our ancestors. Misery has become our water. But now that *your* kind is troubled, you expect everyone to take action." Ria swung back and forth in the air, almost forgetting where she was. "Your kind are greedy and selfish and fickle and sustaining off of the mere after-beams of true light!"

"Watch yourself, fairy!" Argan warned. Her red eyes fixed on Ria and wore no apology.

"Please forgive me, King Grate." Ria bowed to the king before reclaiming her position in the middle. "Human-lover," she muttered in Argan's direction.

"What did you just say?" Argan hissed.

"We've arrived! We're here. Come along." Grate dismounted his sea swallow and wondered if Ria's views were shared by others. He'd attempted to overthrow Dr. Robot years prior but received little support. Plus, the Surges' strength was no match for Robot's technology. Nevertheless, he was going to fight to the finish. *At least I am no coward or traitor, like my father.*

Ria and Argan soon joined Grate's side at the base of the mountain. A waterfall started at the mouth of a cave that sat a half mile up Mount Dejected. It tumbled down the rocky mountainside and dove into the bosom of a choppy river. The water rumbled in a low tone as it flowed away. The three warriors gawked at the size of the mountain. Chilling mist bounced in all directions and clung to their skin. The water was crisp-smelling and reminded one of childhood joys and waking up to the loving aroma of her mother's cooking. Argan scrunched her nose and watched the river. She started to move closer to it.

"I need your help with this, Argan," Grate said while pulling rope from one of the compartments on his saddle. "So, this is the only way to the Moon Fish, huh?"

"Yes. This is it." Ria flew hundreds of feet in the air as she inspected the waterfall.

"I do not like her," Argan said while she assisted Grate with the heavy rope. She still refused to look at him.

"No one is asking you to like her. This is war and we need all of the help we can get."

"We do not need her. Look at her. How useful can she be?"

"Please, Argan. Just... please." Grate tugged on the rope to check for weak areas. He looked worried and aged.

Ria slowly glided back down to them. "I do not envy the wingless. The cave opening is frightfully high."

"And *we* do not envy little—"

"Were you able to see anything up there?" Grate interrupted.

"No..."

"Shame. Let's prepare for the climb then."

"...other than it is all living," added the fairy.

"What?!" Argan exclaimed. "I knew it!" She turned to the river and realized that it had attempted to lure her with its scents.

"Ria, what are you telling us?" Grate dropped the heavy rope.

"The water cascading down the mountain, the vapor, the river... all of it is part of the Living Pools."

Grate peered up at the cave once more.

Argan began to pace. "What should we do, Grate? We are not prepared for this!"

"Are you afraid, mighty Surge?" Ria asked. "I did not come to be indolent. I am prepared, King Grate."

"You can fly! We cannot. The water may turn on us at any moment." She approached Ria and considered using her wave power to remind her that she wasn't the only one gifted by Mother Infinity. "Were you aware that this was a home of the pools?"

"Argan, please. It doesn't matter," Grate calmly reasoned.

"Answer me, Ria!"

"Enough!" he boomed.

Argan's mouth flew open, his tone striking her by surprise.

"The water would've been just as alive even if we had been warned. Let's go. Ria, fly up to the cave and find something on which to secure the rope."

"Yes, king." Ria followed her command and darted upward. Rays of light beamed from her as she flew.

"Argan, keep your mind on the mission."

"This is why no one likes fairies, you know."

"Keep your voice down."

"They are tricky and manipulative and histrionic!" She returned to pacing and rubbed her hands together.

"Then why do you allow her to irk you to this degree?"

"I... I do not know."

"Calm down. All we have to do is find the Moon Fish and ask him to command the water for us."

"Oh, is that all?" She stopped pacing and faced him.

"I'm serious. The queen said he's old and lonely. We'll spend time with him, then he'll want to help. Everyone on the planet wants to get rid of the Robot. That commonality is our key to victory." He used his hand as a visor and checked the distance from the cave once more. "I'm so glad you told me to pack extra rope." He looked at her.

Argan stared into his eyes. She'd always found his naivety and candor to be adorable. After all the danger he'd experienced over the years, it's as though he started each day with a clean slate... believing that the world would ultimately be simple and fair. But it was risky for him to exist in a different world of his own. She just wanted him to be safe. And happy. It was amusing to her when she considered their relationship. How she had him without ever having him. She spent the majority of her time with the king. She slept next to him, ate with him, fought battles with him; and yet, she was unable to have what she wanted more than anything. It pained her in an unexplainable way. These sentiments emerged from an unknown place and she'd gladly rid herself of them if given the chance. It felt like she was suffocating from the agony of it all. She wondered how the Parlimont female looked... and, if *she* were human if he would return the love that she freely offered him.

Grate released a heavy sigh. "I'd like to speak with you, now that we are alone. We haven't gotten an opportunity to discuss what happened last night." He stepped closer to Argan and looked deep into her eyes. "I would like to apologize—"

"There is a large crag resting at the cave entrance!" Ria reported as she crash-landed onto Grate's shoulder. She was winded and sparkling less than usual. "It is an ideal anchor for your climb."

"Are you alright?" Grate asked. He furnished his hand to her so that he could see her better.

"The water... the water was unkind." She transferred to his hand and rested her tired wings.

"Are you hurt?" Argan asked. "Here, have some healing water."

"Thank you. Thank you, Argan. This will be more difficult than I had thought, even with my wings."

Once her bearings were in order, Ria, with rope in hands, pushed upward with all of her strength to reach the mouth of the cave. Bits of the waterfall escaped from the flow and stung her wings in an attempt to deter her; however, she kept going. Waves of pain ran across her body each time the pools came into contact with her. She cried out in distress, yet maintained her grasp on the rope. Argan held her breath as she watched the fairy move upward a foot or two, only to fall back three feet or more.

"This is ludicrous. The rope outweighs her." Grate shielded his eyes from the bright, blue sky as he watched her struggle. "It's alright, Ria!" he yelled. "Pace yourself!"

Ria then changed positions and continued to fly while facing the ground. Her bottom led her as she gripped the rope with her hands as well as feet. Whenever doubt or defeat crept into her mind, she'd think of the unborn young that she secretly carried. Slowly, she made her way to the cave.

"Ahhh! Yes! Yes, Ria!" Grate shouted. He threw his fist in the air in celebration.

Argan leapt for joy and clapped her hands. They were drawn to one another and embraced. The two rocked from side to side. Though unstated, they both knew that their happiness was rooted in more than the fairy's achievement.

"I missed you," whispered Grate. "Please forgive me."

After reaching her destination, Ria peered on from above and rested. "Bring the healing water with you!" Ria yelled. Her belly rumbled. "And some of those water berries, too please!"

"Did she just ask for berries?" Grate laughed, still holding Argan.

With the rope secured around the crag, Ria gave them clearance to begin the climb. Grate yanked the rope; then suspended his legs as he hung from it for a few seconds to test its strength. They were to ascend the mountainside only several feet from the lively waterfall. Its rumbling was getting louder as its attention was now focused on the two. The water's color began to darken to a royal blue.

"This looks good. We can do this. I'll start, and you shadow me. If you can handle it." He winked at Argan.

She rolled her eyes in jest. They both knew she was the stronger one. He stretched his neck, back, and limbs before jumping into the air to grab the rope as high as possible. His feet slid against the slippery rock. Without looking down or thinking about how far he had to go, Grate began to scale the mountain. He committed to a rhythm and was surprised by how well he was doing. Without hesitation, Argan soon followed. She used her feet and hands to assist as she braced herself for the unexpected. Grate peeked below to his right.

"Not too bad, right?" he asked confidently.

However, the instant he looked up, a portion of the waterfall berated him and sprayed across his face. The water was like scalding sand and wiping his eyes only made it worse. Grate's head flew back, which caused him to lose balance. Argan waved in his direction in an attempt to push his foot closer to the slick foundation, but this only resulted in him running mid-air. Grate tried to compose himself; but the severe pain in his eyes made him panic. He panted in fear as his heavy legs hung beneath him.

"Calm yourself and keep climbing, Grate! We have to keep climbing!"

Just then, parts of the fall froze and darted toward Argan. Pellets of ice punished her and attacked her entire left side. She knew that the relentless Living Pools would intensify, regardless of what she said or did. The air that once smelled of cheery memories had been replaced by a zesty, unpleasant odor.

"Climb, Grate! No matter what! Climb!" she grimaced.

"Hold on! I need to rest," Grate announced.

"Let me know when you want to continue!" Replied Argan. A drop of blood fell from her brow and stung her eye.

Grate hugged the rope and laid his head upon his clenched fists. Barbs of ice began to attack him without pause. He didn't want to climb anymore; but, he also didn't want to return to the ground. He thought of the Old World and his mother. He thought of his father and wondered why he'd chosen Parlimont's son over him. He wondered if his grandmother was well. And then, he remembered the light from his dream. A boost of foreign energy instantly welled up inside him. And with his eyes shut tightly, he resumed his climb.

"Argan!"

"Yes, King?"

"Let's climb!"

The ice pellets turned into icicles and kept pursuing the pair. The rope became more difficult to grip as the slick ice clung to it. They wrapped the rope around their hands to keep from slipping. Ria timidly pleaded with the falls from up above; but, it was unproductive. The two howled out in misery as they were pounded by the raging pools.

"Why are you doing this?! What have we done?" Grate pleaded.

"Do not interact with them!" warned Argan.

The icicles rounded into hail balls. The stinging pricks immediately turned into burdensome blows. After one of them struck his temple, Grate opened his eyes and briefly saw four fists holding the rope in front of him instead of two. He shook his head and held on even tighter. Ice flakes gathered in his hair and eyebrows. Argan waved once at her attackers and was met with a sickening blow to the belly. Bloody saliva fell from her lips as she curled around the rope and turned her back to the waterfall. They'd both stopped climbing and hung, suspended in the air, as the water had its way with them.

"Oh, please leave them alone! They mean no harm!" Ria cried. "You are killing them!" Ria covered her face as she couldn't stand to watch any more.

Which came first? The water or the light? It was a question as old as Mother Infinity herself. There was an unspoken respect that the two sources had for each other; as water could drown out light and light could dry up water.

Ria felt tiny kicks inside of her belly. She knew the gravity of what she was considering. She also knew that Grate and Argan would not make it up to the cave unless the water showed mercy. The thought of future generations being forced to live beneath the glass barrier was unfathomable. Her mouth went dry as she started to speak.

"Living Pools!" Ria shouted. With a gust of vigor, she shot up above the waterfall and faced the mouth of the cave. "I… Renounce… My… LIGHT!"

All at once, the water stood still. The waterfall suspended in the air. Even the drops that had strayed away, halted in their place. The torrid river below also paused.

Ria stood tall as she hovered thousands of feet in the air.

Grate opened one eye. Then he opened the other.

"Oh, no," Argan barely said .

"Whoa. What happened?" Grate looked around. "Argan?"

"Climb, Grate!"

"Huh?"

"CLIMB!" Argan's ruby-colored eyes bulged at the king.

Ria outstretched her arms and turned left toward the pink and auburn evening sky. A stream of water hungrily crept from the cave and extended in the fairy's direction. It defied gravity as it passed the motionless waterfall and reached to meet her. Ria closed her eyes. Her nostrils flared as she attempted to control her breathing. Looking more like a finger than anything else, the stream finally met the fire fairy, and connected to her feet. Her light blue shimmers pulsated in the air and shone throughout the water that latched onto her. The glittering lights traveled through the water and into the cave. The fairy's cyan blue body paled to white and began to expand. Slowly, her light darkened to a brownish yellow, then turned to orange, and finally deepened red. By this point, Ria's glow had doubled in size. The water crawled up her body and covered every part of her. The swelling red glow spread into the Living Pools, including the waterfall and river.

Grate and Argan continued to climb. He glanced at the now bright red water that reflected across his face and knew that whatever was occurring had Argan petrified. He could hear her panting behind him. She prayed aloud in an ancient language that he could never manage to master. His shoulders burned terribly, and his abs ached from being tensed for so long. His hands were raw and worn, but he ignored it all and kept going. The water's fragrance had neutralized and gave off no odor.

Bright purple wing-like rays branched from the fairy's red core. The rays sizzled and cracked while her glowing shell continued to expand. Memories of her racing through the boundless water and enjoying the entire planet played through Ria's mind as her shell separated into different colored layers. Vivid rings of carmine, sapphirine, jade, and amber emerged from the bloated red ball of fire. Whistling sailed through the wind as wisps of golden light emerged from the spectacle's outer layers. Nearby Living Pools mirrored this light and absorbed it all. Suddenly, the center of the ball turned bright white, and its surrounding layers dissipated. Ria held her belly with both hands. Tears streamed down her face and she exhaled; relieved.

"Goodbye, Ria," whispered Argan.

In that moment, an earsplitting clap radiated through The Stretch. The fairy's white light faded to black and the pools began to flow again.

Chapter Eighteen: The Moon Fish

Grate and Argan stood at the entrance of the cave and drenched themselves with healing strongwater. The water flow beside them was satiated and slow-moving. It didn't even notice that the two were in the cave. Grate looked at the open space in which Ria had hovered and disappeared and wondered what he'd just witnessed. He turned to Argan.

"Is Ria... gone?" he asked.

"She is." Argan shook her head in disbelief. "That was the most courageous act I have ever witnessed."

"She will be missed. To Ria..." Grate lifted his canteen in memorial.

"To Ria..."

The two took a sip from the canteen, then carefully followed the path of the water in hopes of not disturbing it. It was a sobering moment for them both; being so close to death yet, being granted the opportunity to continue with life.

"Hello!" a small voice echoed through the cave. "Wait for me!"

A flickering, orange light approached them from the cave opening.

"Ria?!" Grate said with hope.

"I do not think so," Argan cautiously replied.

Once the orange spot drew closer, they realized that it was indeed a fire fairy; although, not Ria.

"Hello, King Grate. Hello, Argan." The fairy fluttered around them and smiled.

"Jinxt?" Grate asked.

"Lucille Two," insisted the fairy.

"Hi, Lucille Two," Argan sighed and rubbed the goosebumps that had formed on her arms.

"The fire fairies said that you would be in this cave," squeaked Lucille Two.

"You have found us. Is something the matter?" Argan asked,ever wary of all around her.

"No. It smells horrible here," said Lucille Two with a sniff.

"I hadn't noticed before now," responded Grate. "What *is* that?"

"We must continue, the water will not be satisfied for long." Argan ignored the question and looked down at the source of the waterfall. Traces of Ria's light twinkled within the currents.

"May I join you?" Lucille Two fluttered before Grate.

"Are you sure? It's dangerous," he answered.

"Yes, I am sure."

"Alright then. We are to follow the path of the water. It will lead us to the Moon Fish," Argan said with urgency. "We should not stop anymore."

The three hurried through the twisting cave and were careful to avoid the water. When it became increasingly difficult to see in the darkness, Grate removed some flare bark from the satchel that he was wearing and passed one to Argan and kept one for himself. The bark lit like torches upon bending them until they cracked. Lucille Two helped in her own way by intensifying her fairy light.

A putrid smell stung their noses and worsened; the deeper they traveled into the cave. Grate's eyes began to tear up from the odor, so he tied a piece of cloth around the lower half of his face while being careful not to burn himself with the flame. He also noticed that the tranquil stream was becoming more animated and starting to reach for him.

"Faster," Grate commanded as he wanted to avoid the Living Pools at all cost. The thick, foul air lodged in his throat and caused him to choke.

"I will lead," offered Argan, who was less affected by the worsening smell. "Yiiiipe!" she hollered.

"Are you alright?" Grate asked.

"It bit me!" she answered as she momentarily hopped on one leg. It felt like her foot had been sliced by razors.

The pools splashed against the walls of the cave and began to darken in color.

"Shame on you!" buzzed Lucille two. "These are fine creatures! They mean well and want the best for the land just as we do. We all wish to be reunited with the outside pools. Do not punish them!" She pointed at the water, causing it to wither in embarrassment.

The choppy stream had relaxed and become a thin ribbon of water. Grate and Argan stared at Lucille Two in wonderment as she looked back at them with her head cocked to the side in confusion.

"King Grate, what will the air breathers do once the barrier is no more?"

"I haven't figured out that part, my friend," he sighed.

"You will die if you cannot breathe."

"Hold on. You can speak to the Living Pools?" Argan asked.

"Yes."

"You should have told us!"

"You should have asked."

"Will you please ask the pools to join us in battle then?"

"No."

"And why not?" Argan squinted at the fairy.

"They are my friends. Friends may offer their life in battle but should never be expected to do so."

Grate placed his hand on Argan's shoulder, who was prepared to argue. Time had taught them that it was impossible to change the shifter's mind.

"Let's continue," he advised. "Please light the way, Lucille Two."

The cave became darker and more humid as they proceeded. Argan and Grate had begun to relax since the Living Pools were no longer a threat and Lucille Two brightly floated along in silence. The only issue was that the cave reeked of rotten flesh and mildew, although there appeared to be only rock and water present.

"Who goes there?!" a congested voice boomed from an inner cave.

The entire mountain seemed to tremble at the sound. The king and Surge quickly turned to Lucille Two for guidance.

"It is the Moon Fish," she said.

After they came a few more steps closer, the voice roared out once more.

"Who is here?! Answer me!"

By this time, the surrounding water had become agitated and ran up the cave walls as a warning to the visitors. Grate and Argan looked at one another, and then at Lucille Two. She shrugged. Grate swallowed hard before lifting the cloth and partially cupping his hand around his mouth to amplify his voice.

"I am King Grate! I come in peace with my friends, Argan and Lucille Two!" he yelled into the darkness.

"Ha! Names do nothing for me!" huffed the voice. "You are who you are without the names your mothers gave you!"

The fetid smell worsened. Lucille Two nodded then took a seat on Argan's shoulder. Grate crouched down in an attempt to see through the blackness but saw nothing. Next, he motioned for the others to follow him. With a torch in one hand and weapon in the other, he ignored the water that nipped at his legs and began to run. Argan followed suit, but crashed into him after he abruptly stopped at the sight of the Moon Fish.

"Sorry," he voiced without thought. Grate stood, stunned, with his eyes wide with astonishment.

Before them sat a gargantuan, beige, gossamer-skinned fish. It was round and fat and nearly twelve feet tall and wide. Its features were similar to those of a human, with a long, flabby nose and fleshy, pouty lips. Its large, dark eyes were covered by skin and weren't useful for seeing. It sat in a small pool of water and had been trapped in place for the last twenty-three years. Living Pools flowed underneath the fish and filtered through its gills. Despite there being a lack of food and proper water supply, the greasy–looking fish had been sustained. Its miniature fins protruded from its face on both sides and looked more like ears.

"Come no closer!" advised the fish. "WHO GOES THERE?!" Its breath was nauseating.

Grate dropped his head for a moment and regained his poise. Lucille Two tried to wave the odor away from her nose, then whispered something to Argan.

"SPEAK!"

Grate stepped forward. "Before you stand Argan, the core guardian, Lucille, the shifter, and Grate, the human—"

"Air breather?!" With that, the Moon fish coughed and hawked a ball of salty, noxious slime in his direction, causing the three to take cover.

"How dare you enter my domain?! Nothing is sacred to you filthy varmints and everything that you touch turns to sand!" it heaved and spat again.

Grate slung the slime from his body and retrieved his morning star from the ground. The weapon was dripping with sticky muck. Lucille Two, who'd been slammed against the cave wall by the mucus, flew around in a daze. She then shook herself and approached the giant fish.

"Excuse me, my name is Lucille Two; and not Lucille. Lucille is the human girl from The Community."

"Death to all humans!" exclaimed the fish as it prepared to spit again.

The pool below began to darken and rouse.

"No, please!" cried Argan as she dodged the mucus missiles. "We were told to come to you, All Powerful One!"

"To come to *me*? Ha! And why is that?" smiled the fish.

The pool's color returned to light blue and began to sprout around the Moon Fish like a fountain. It elaborately spurted from all sides and daintily fell to the ground. Lucille Two twinkled and clapped her hands, pleased.

Argan, leery of the water, inched closer to the fish. "Um... we were told to find you because you are so wise and thoughtful. And because you want the best for this place," she continued.

"Indeed. This is true. I also want the best for myself. Ha! Why have you brought an air breather along? They are nothing but trouble."

"He is a good human."

"Hmph! That is like saying one has a *good* parasite! A *good* sadness. A *good* burden. A *good* mistake. How does that serve any purpose? Ha!"

"I agree. I will keep my eye on him."

Lucille Two examined Grate and shrugged.

"What do you desire from me, madam?" said the fish. "I have not had a visitor in more than eight cycles. Ha! I am interested to know why you have decided to come now. Have I forgotten a holiday?" he chuckled.

Lucille Two smiled.

"We were informed by trustworthy sources that you have a unique bond with the Living Pools—"

"I do! They are my best friends. A rare benefit and insufferable affliction. Ha! They keep me alive... just enough for me to wish to perish. I am sure that you can relate, core guardian... to having a friend like that... considering the company you keep. Ha!"

Grate scoffed.

"Tread lightly, air breather!" the Moon Fish warned.

"We have been told," continued Argan, "that you could advise us on how to capture some of it. Some of the Living Pools."

"What?!" The fish started to laugh. It laughed and laughed. And laughed until it began to cough and brown mucous seeped from the corners of its mouth.

The now golden water sloshed against itself. Lucille Two giggled and swirled in the air.

Grate thought of their mission and wondered if the baby was safe. "Will you help us, Moon Fish?" he asked.

Lucille Two stopped her dancing and quickly flew over to him. She looked him in the eyes. "He does not like humans, King Grate. Have you not noticed? It would be wise to allow Argan address him. Wisdom is better than pride."

Grate bit his bottom lip in frustration.

"Will you help us, merciful Moon Fish?" Argan asked.

"I have not decided," he answered. "I have enjoyed the company... of yours and the shifter's. Ha! What if I help you if you help me?"

Grate looked at Argan with raised eyebrows and nodded.

"How may we help you, Great One?" she asked with the most humble tone she could muster.

"I have been craving the root of the thicket patch for decades now," the fish drooled. "It is at the base of this cave. Retrieve some and bring it back to me. Then I will assist you."

Grate motioned for Argan to come to him. "What do you think?" he asked.

"I do not trust it," Argan replied.

"What other option do we have?" concluded Grate.

Argan turned toward the great fish. "Your Excellency, do we have your word that you will help us?"

The Moon Fish gave another thunderous laugh. His blubbery body jiggled and caused the ground to shake beneath them. "What leverage do you have? Ha! I did not invade *your* home seeking guidance. Retrieve the root or do not retrieve the root. I will be here," he huffed.

"Ask it to control the pools," Grate whispered.

"The pools are no longer concerned with you! Ha!"

They'd underestimated the fish's keen sense of hearing. Lucille Two waved goodbye to the blind Moon Fish as they headed back to the opening of the cave. And as the giant had assured, the Living Pools didn't bother them at all, which made the trip down the mountain relatively easy. Argan began the descent first, Grate followed, and Lucille Two maintained her fairy form and reached the bottom before anyone else. She fluttered above the neighboring river and suddenly shifted into a Moon Fish. Water splashed as her massive body crashed into it.

"Feed me thicket patch roots! Ha!" she teased. "Yum, yum, yum!"

Relieved to be on the ground again, Argan played along and tossed invisible roots in Lucille Two's direction. The surrounding pools ignored them and continued to flow as usual.

"Argan, where is your sea swallow?" Grate asked as he removed the cloth from around his nose. "Stop playing around, you two. Something's wrong."

He reached for his weapon and began to jog around the mountain in search of the missing animal. After running for a few minutes, Grate found himself face-to-face with a gigantic eel creature. It smiled to show hundreds of jagged clear teeth.

"I come in peace," Grate offered as the eel whipped its spiny tail in his direction.

With a loud snap, electric waves sprang from the eel and knocked Grate onto his back.

"Grate!" Argan cried from behind. Her fiery, red eyes stayed fixed on the eel. Shortly after, Lucille Two, who'd returned to her fairy form, joined them.

"Stay… stay back, Lucille…" uttered the groggy king. He blinked his eyes and tried to focus. He touched his nose as it started to bleed.

"FACE ME!" roared the eel.

"With pleasure…" Argan quickly helped Grate to an upright position then charged toward the eel at full speed.

The eel chuckled and used the same defense as before; but, this time, Argan waved her arm in his direction to repel the electric current and send it back to him.

"Aaaargh!" the eel cried as he crashed into the thicket patch that was behind him.

Without hesitation, Argan leapt into the air and pounced onto the eel. With mighty blows using her arms, elbows, and forehead, she struck him over and over. Each time that the eel would attempt to use his tail to shock her, Argan would deflect the waves. The eel writhed and squirmed beneath the merciless Surge. Lucille Two punched the air and cheered from the side.

"Enough! Enough!" pleaded the battered eel. "Please! I have no more fight left in me!"

After smacking him across the face one last time, Argan climbed off the eel and caught her breath. She wiped her mouth with the back of her hand and checked on Grate. "How are you, my king?"

"I am frine... fyine... fine." Grate was now standing and struggled to keep his balance.

"You are injured!" Lucille Two pointed toward his midsection.

Grate looked down to find the vest he wore stained with blood. The eel's electric wave had split his side open. He applied pressure to the wound and staggered a bit. His ears were still ringing, and his fingers were tingling.

"Grate!" Argan darted to his side just as his legs gave out beneath him. Her hands trembled as she fumbled with his leather satchel to retrieve the bottle of strongwater. She quickly lifted his vest to expose the gash in his side and poured the remaining healing water across his left side and abdomen.

"Shame on you!" scolded Lucille Two. She'd reached the eel, who was still lying on the ground, and hovered above him. "We are on a mission to save the land and you have only delayed us!"

"I am sorry. I... I truly am!" gave the exhausted creature. "I saw the air breather and was overcome with rage. I am the last of my kind because of the humans. They have killed my entire family. There is no one left!" he cried.

"That is horrible!" Lucille Two exclaimed. "There, there..."

"It was not *this* human!" insisted Argan. "How are you, Grate?"

"I'll be alright. Just let me rest."

"We are here to gather some of those roots," Argan gestured behind the eel. "And then we will be on our way. Let me by."

"What is your mission?" The eel rose from the ground.

Argan's eyes began to glow and turn red once more.

"Please, I will keep to myself," he assured.

"Right now," Argan grunted as she dug into the thick soil to expose the root, "it is to take some of *this* back up the mountain. Afterward, we will destroy the human that is responsible for all of the wrong on this planet. The violence. The killing. The barrier. All of it."

"Please, let me help you, madam." With little effort, the eel wrapped his large tail around the thicket bush and pulled it from the ground. He gave a few hard shakes to remove the chunks of dirt that clung to it, then snapped the root from the rest of the bush.

"Thank you..." Argan wrapped her arms around the massive plant and held it in front of her. She studied him and wondered if he was trying to trick her.

"It is the least that I can do." The eel repeated the act a few more times and placed each root at Argan's feet. "I am very sorry for attacking your human."

"He is not *my* human. He is my king."

"I am sorry for attacking him," he gave while turning to Grate, "Your Majesty, please accept my most sincere apology for my offense."

"All is forgotten," Grate said with a tired smile. The truth was that he honestly couldn't remember anything after meeting the Moon Fish. He scratched the tip of his nose then looked at Argan. "We must be going now."

"I would like to join you!" blurted the eel. "I would be of great use. I promise not to get in the way. And it would appease my broken heart to have the opportunity to avenge the deaths of my family members. I need this... please... please."

Argan and Grate stared at one another. Argan shrugged. Next, Lucille Two fluttered closer to the king and whispered into his ear.

"Let him come, King Grate! He has a good heart. And for where we are going, one had better have lots of good heart."

Grate nodded. "What's your name, sir?"

"Ker," he beamed. "My name is Ker and I am glad to join your team."

"The pleasure is ours as well. Stay at the base of the mountain and watch our swallow while we take this up. Our other one seems to have wandered away," Grate said while scratching his cheek.

"Yes, King... about that. I must also apologize for having the first swallow for dinner. If it is any consolation, it was neither tender nor tasty. I travel incredibly fast and can serve as a fine substitute, if anyone wants a ride."

Argan and King Grate tied the massive roots to their backs and prepared for the climb. As planned, Ker remained at the foot of Mount Dejected while the other three returned to the Moon Fish. This time, the fish didn't yell upon their arrival. In fact, he was fast asleep and snoring so loudly that the entire cave rumbled, causing dust and pebbles to fall from above.

"I believe that he has gone into hibernation," Argan whispered. "Excuse me! Moon Fish!"

"Wha-What?! What is it now?" coughed the fish. "What took you so long?"

Argan rolled her eyes. "We humbly apologize. We have brought the root as you requested."

"Ha! Well? What is keeping you?!" The Moon Fish opened its wide mouth as far as it would stretch. It was an incredible sight. They could see shadows of is internal organs past its large, flat tongue. The stench was almost unbearable; and between that and extraordinary view, both Grate and Argan were unable to move.

"AAAARRRGGGH!" roared the impatient fish.

"Uh, quickly! Untie the roots!" Argan grabbed the torch that Grate was holding; then turned her back to him so that he could access the roots that were strapped to her.

Using a small knife that he kept in his boot, he cut the rope and let the large bundle fall to the ground. Then Argan returned the torch to him.

"Where is Ji—Lucille Two?!" Grate looked around.

Argan hurled the heavy roots into the fish's mouth, then picked up more. "What?!" Her beating heart distracted her. "Turn around!" She snapped the ropes with her hands and wasted no time in tossing the remainder of the roots into the Moon Fish's mouth.

"*There* you are!" Grate stooped down to the cave floor and gently picked up the fairy, who had fainted. "Hey! Hey now…" he whispered.

Lucille Two batted her eyes. "It reeks here, King Grate."

"War is tough, my dear friend. Pull yourself together," he smiled.

"That is all of it!" Argan shouted.

The fish sat there, frozen with its mouth still ajar. Argan turned to Grate with a helpless look- then noticed Lucille Two. "Oh, stars no… what happened?"

Suddenly, the Moon fish shut its mouth with a deafening clap. Grate cradled Lucille Two and covered Argan with his body as they fell to the wet floor.

"Mmmmmm! Ha!" The fish moaned and smacked with delight. "Mmmmmmm! More!"

"We have no more!" Argan stood to her feet.

Lucille Two had regained the strength to fly again.

"MORE!"

"There is no more! Please…"

Grate touched Argan's arm and stepped ahead of her. "Moon Fish, now that you have eaten, will you help us as you promised?"

"Who do you think you are, air breather?! Ha! You dare approach *me* and make demands, while you have no leverage? No power!" It spat a huge glob of mucus in his direction.

Grate ducked to dodge it. The water that spouted around the fish changed from light green to dark blue.

"*That* is what I think of you, your mission, and anyone who associates with you! I would rather shrivel up and DIE before helping the likes of you! Now go! Leave this place!"

"We'll go—"

"GO!"

The surrounding pools turned a deep, midnight blue. The waters swirled and swelled then immediately rushed toward the three.

"Ahahahahaha!" The fish's laugh echoed through the caves as Argan, Grate, and Lucille Two fled as fast as they could.

Their flesh burned as drops of water contacted their bodies. The pools crashed against the cave walls and curled and foamed, in search of its prey. Grate and Argan's feet and ankles felt as if they were being ripped apart as the pools began to flood the caves. They could see moonlight at the mouth ahead and knew that this was the end. Their hearts raced for they realized that they wouldn't have time to climb down the rope *and* escape the fury of the raging pools.

"What do we do, Grate?!" Argan's voice shook.

"We die with pride," Grate voiced.

Argan swallowed hard and nodded.

"This is it," he said before taking her by the hand. "I love you."

They ran even faster and pushed off of the ledge and sprang from the mountain's side enough to avoid the falls. Dark blue pools spurted out after them and laughed. The ravenous waters waited below.

"Nooooo!" howled Ker, the eel, as he watched Argan and Grate fall through the air.

Lucille Two, who'd been floating above near the cave's opening, calmly leaned forward and rolled herself into a ball. She continued to spin, faster and faster, until she was nearly invisible. Then with lightning speed, she plunged into the rowdy waterfall and reappeared as an oversized, winged reptile that had a large, orange beak. She was now rust-colored and ferocious; and had a throat pouch, similar to that of an earthly pelican. She zoomed through the air to catch Argan and Grate just before they'd reached the lethal river. They fell onto her wide, scaly back with a thud. The waters below boiled up toward Lucille Two's tan belly and cursed at her for spoiling their fun. Grate and Argan clung to each other in disbelief as they glided down to safety.

"My stars, I thought that everything was over!" Argan whispered.

"We owe you our lives, Jinxt!" Grate proclaimed.

Lucille Two landed, with ample space between them and the Living Pools to allow Grate and Argan to hop down from her back. Argan whimpered as she leaned against the king and looked down at her leg. The pools had eaten through her right calf muscle; leaving her unable to walk.

"That was unbelievable!" Ker exclaimed as he rushed to them. "I-I-I am speechless! I truly believed that you were falling to your deaths. And shifter, you are a hero! You are nothing short of wonderful!"

Grate nervously searched through his satchel and retrieved the bottle of healing water, only to remember that they'd used the last of it earlier.

"Emmmm!" Lucille Two said with a closed beak. She craned her long neck and looked at the bottle in Grate's hand. "Emmmm!"

"What do you want? There are only drops left," Grate replied as he shook his head.

"I am unable to walk. We must stop the bleeding. What shall I do, Grate?" Argan's worried eyes stared at her leg in disbelief.

"Shhhh. Stay calm." Grate ripped the cloth he had from earlier and packed it into her open wound. He used the rest of it to tie around her leg, directly under her knee.

"Emmmmm!" Lucille Two repeated. She moved closer to Grate.

"It seems that she wants the bottle, Your Majesty," suggested Ker.

With a few quick spins, Lucille Two transformed into Lucille, the human girl. She pointed to the bottle and gestured for him to remove its top.

Argan's mouth flew open. Grate stared at her; unable to move.

"Woah!" Ker gasped and appeared as if he might faint.

Lucille Two shrugged her shoulders and politely removed the bottle top before spitting a mouthful of Living Pool water into it. She quickly placed her small hand over it and replaced the top before any of it could wonder off. She smiled. "I am sorry about your leg, Argan. You need strongwater."

"Jinxt?" Grate's voice shook. He had so many questions. His mind was cloudy with the traffic of recent events. He was shocked that she'd trapped the water... but even more so relieved. He was also confused by her human form. "Have you been to The Community?! It's unsafe there. What have we told you?" He knelt on one knee and embraced the girl. "And *thank* you. *Thank* you for the Living Pools!"

"No," she said.

"No?" Grate stood.

"I have not been to The Community."

Grate gave a concerned look. "Then how did you see the girl?"

Lucille Two explained how she'd met Lucille. She told them about the twin boys, the lost map, and all she knew of Dr. Parlimont's plan to kidnap the babies from The Community. She also told them how she managed to capture some of The Living Pools.

"I did not capture them. The notion that they are all one life form is incorrect. Much of the pools desire to rejoin the waters that rest beyond the barrier. The Living Pools in this area are more aggressive and resentful. But the curious pools that reside closer to your caves and near The Community are more reasonable."

"This is so perplexing!" Ker announced. "I do not understand. Are you telling me that the human responsible for all of this mayhem is *also* targeting humans?"

"Yes. There is no limit to his madness," Grate answered. "Lucille Two, take winged form again and fly to the Onyx Caves to fetch a container of healing water. Tell them that I sent you. Also, get a report of how my grandmother is doing."

Lucille Two nodded.

"Then meet us at the green area of the planet. We will be at the largest home there. It sits on a hill. Trust no one once you are near the humans. Do you understand?"

Lucille Two nodded again.

"Good. Do everything with haste!"

Chapter Nineteen: Need and Want

Grate and Argan mounted the remaining sea swallow and raced through The Stretch en route to Parlimont Manor. Ker's endurance and speed surprised them, as he was able to keep up with them. They dashed by hills, trees, and a school of land fish. They even passed the aqua-deer buck for which Grate had been hunting all season. But there was no time for that.

"Argan, how are you?" asked Grate, who was riding in front and holding the reigns.

Her body rested on his. "I am weak and still losing blood."

"Lucille Two will meet us soon. Just hold on."

"King?"

"Yes? What's the matter?"

"I was wondering about our war plan."

"Do not fret."

"Well, I will worry less if I know what you have in mind," she said with her chin on his shoulder.

"Our plan is to go to Parlimont Manor, pick up the baby, and bring it back with us. Please rest now."

"Is that all?" Argan asked.

"What do you mean?"

"So... we are to rush in, grab the baby, take it to the caves, and then what?"

"Anyone else from the household, who may want to join us can come along as well."

"And what of Doctor Robot? When do we face him?"

"Excuse me," Ker panted. "What baby?"

"There has got to be more. You know this. He could be at the home this very instant. We must be prepared for that," Argan continued.

"Um, pardon me... again...what is special about this one baby? Whose baby is it?" Ker slithered closer to them and waited. "Is it a male or female human? Not that that detail matters, of course."

"It is imperative that we proceed with a proper plan," Argan insisted as Grate slowed the sea swallow.

"Are we stopping? Why are we stopping, Your Majesty?" asked Ker.

"Would you mind giving us a moment of privacy, please?" Argan gently touched the eel's face.

"Yes madam. Of course."

"Grate, what is wrong? Talk to me. I have never seen you like this. Why does your mind wander so?"

Grate shrugged.

"Talk to me. This is life or death you know..."

"Do you think that I am unaware?!" he questioned, still facing forward. "Do you think that for one second, I take this situation lightly?!" He dismounted the sea swallow and walked away for a moment.

Argan glanced over at Ker then lowered her eyes in shame.

Grate returned to Argan and punched his palm. "For the first time in my life, I don't know what to do. There. I said it. I don't know what to do, Argan! I am taxed with such responsibility, but feel that no matter what I choose, I'll be defeated."

Tears streamed from Argan's eyes.

"What will I do with a baby?" Grate dropped his head in dismay.

"Oh, Grate. How did this happen? Well, I know how it happened. But how could you be so irresponsible?"

"It wasn't under my control."

"Nonsense. You are always in control."

"Not this time." He spat and kicked at the ground.

"Are you sure that—"

"It's my baby, Argan. I can feel it. I'm sure."

A disappointed Argan thought for a moment. "Listen, we will rescue the baby and return to the caves if that pleases you. And if Robot and his men are there, we will deal with them as well. And anyone who stands in our way for that matter. This is war. Perhaps we should call our warriors to attack with us and kill any human that stands in our way—" She stopped. "Oh stars, your father will be there," she uttered.

"Yes," Grate said while staring at the ground.

"How long has it been since you have seen each other?"

"Since I was a boy."

"Do you think that he will be on our side?"

"I do not know. I have so many unanswered questions."

"The two of you must talk. He is your fath—"

"Is everything alright over there?" Ker interrupted from afar.

"I don't want to talk to my father, Argan."

"A conversation is needed between the two of you. It has been too long, Grate. I would do anything to speak with my father again. Enough is enough!"

Chapter Twenty: Twenty-four Years Prior During the Incident

On the night of Steddy's fortieth birthday, he received an alarming call from his attorney.

"Mister Watters, it's time," trembled the voice. The attorney cleared his throat and continued. "A helicopter will be there shortly to pick you all up and take you to the launch site as planned. Your family and friends are being contacted as we speak. Do you have the tickets?"

"Yes, of course!" Steddy blurted.

"Godspeed, Mister Watters."

Steddy raced to his office and removed the family portrait from the wall. His hands twitched as he turned the dial from left to right, then back left to unlock the safe. It popped open to reveal a flashing red button and a small stack of black credit card-looking tickets. He took a deep breath. The flashing light further confirmed that it was finally happening. Steddy quickly secured the tickets in his wallet and rushed to his bedroom to find his wife and five-year-old son asleep.

"Julia. Honey, wake up!" Steddy sat on the bed next to her and leaned down to whisper in her ear.

She smelled of sweet memories and hope. He placed his large hand on her round, pregnant belly and realized how truly afraid he was.

"Julia… Julia… Baby!" he said more firmly until she awoke. "I got the call. Let's go!" Steddy jogged to the other side of the bed to pick up their sleeping boy.

Julia's cheeks flushed red as she leaned over to grab her shades from the nightstand and felt around for her support cane. Steddy rushed to her and grabbed her arm; then led her to their rooftop to meet the helicopter.

Once on the roof and inside the helicopter, the Watters family fastened their seatbelts and prepared to take flight. Steddy texted his sister, Corrine, to make sure that she and their mother were on the way to the Parlimont spacecraft.

"What's wrong mommy? Don't cry," said an innocent voice. Young Grate rubbed his mother's belly and spoke to it. "We're going to outer *spates*, sister!"

Julia lifted her glasses to wipe her tears and smiled. "Thank you, baby. Mommy's alright."

Steddy took Julia's hand and softly kissed it. "Everything will be okay. Capiche?"

"Si, capisco," she chuckled and let out a heavy sigh.

"I have to go potty," Grate said with big eyes and a bashful smile.

"You don't need to hold it this time, Big Man," Steddy assured. "That's why mommy put a diaper on you tonight."

"It's warm!" Grate giggled. He leaned against his mother and placed his thumb in his mouth.

A few states away, in the middle of the dessert, waited the massive Parlimont space shuttle on its launch pad.

Doctor Hampton Parlimont waited onboard in a luxury suite. He checked his watch. "This is it, Junior. This is the day," he sighed. "Today I become God!"

Six year-old Hampton Junior was sitting on the floor watching videos on a handheld device with little Garla Lastoré, who was about the same age. They paid no mind to Hampton Senior. The father and son weren't emotionally close, despite the amount of time that they'd been spending together.

Dr. Parlimont glanced down at his watch again before rolling to the bathroom to take his evening medicine. He loathed taking the injection and thirteen pills. He'd been sickly his entire life, but seemed to have severely declined in health as a result of his wife's death. His heart had become weak and caused him to suffer many related complications.

Mrs. Elizabeth Parlimont had passed away during childbirth a year prior. She was an incredibly kind and humble person a as well as notable concert pianist. Parlimont, now obsessed with immortality and bringing the dead back to life, spent the majority of the day in his lab experimenting and researching. The last ounce of humanity that Dr. Parlimont possessed, died along with his wife and he'd become even more insufferable than before— to the point that he couldn't keep a nanny... or a friend.

A knock at his cabin door caused Dr. Parlimont to toss the remaining pills back into the dispenser.

"Ah! Right on schedule," he said as he adjusted his legs in his wheelchair and sat erect. "Come in!" he sang.

One of the guards entered to notify him that the Brooks family had just boarded the ship. Pastor Randolph Brooks, his wife, Emersyn, and their toddler, Serenity, were the guests of honor. After the passing of his wife, Dr. Parlimont turned to faith when he felt as though he was on the brink of losing his mind. Pastor Brooks spent countless hours over the phone supporting the heartbroken man. Parlimont joined their church as a "remote" member and donated millions of dollars to their ministry. He respected the Brooks and their good works immensely; so much that he welcomed them onto the spacecraft free of charge.

"Knock, knock!" Pastor Brooks's kind voice called out from behind the guard. "Hey, Doctor P! We just wanted to let you know that we made it safely and are tremendously grateful for everything!" He approached Dr. Parlimont with a sincere smile and offered his hand for a shake.

"It's no problem at all. It is my pleasure to have you and your family aboard! I can rest easy knowing that one of God's favorites is here!"

"Ah, no, no...please. I am merely His servant. A messenger!"

"All I can say is job well done, Pastor. Thank you."

"This is a great looking machine! Wow!"

"A lot of hard work went into this. I'm very proud."

"As you should be, Doc. Hey, Hamp Junior! How's it going, buddy?"

"The cartoons have all of his attention, you see."

"Indeed! Serenity enjoys the one with the talking fruit and vegetables. What will they think of next, right?! And who is *this* little princess over here?"

"That's Garla Lastoré. Brianca Lastoré's child."

"Ah, yes. Very sad. She seemed to be a beautiful soul. It's incredible that you've adopted her."

"Ehh," Dr. Parlimont shrugged. "Brianca chose to discontinue the treatment. Why anyone would opt to die is beyond me. It's just stupid. Also, I'm not adopting Garla. Just rearing her along with Junior. I can barely keep up with the one that I have, what will I do with two crumb-snatchers?" he laughed.

"Right…" Pastor Brooks said with a stunned expression. "Well, let us know if there's anything we can do. Serenity would love a playmate!"

"Here, take her! Take her!" Parlimont said before turning to the girl. "Do you want to go live with the Brookses?" He slapped his knee and laughed.

Pastor Brooks took a deep breath and reminded himself that everyone was worth patience and a chance at redemption. "Okay, Doctor P, I need to be getting back to Sister Brooks and my little pumpkin. But, I want to say a quick prayer with you before I go."

Hours later, the Watters family arrived at the launch site and met up with their immediate and extended family members, as well as close friends. They grouped together for a joint, mass prayer then turned to Steddy for guidance. He distributed the black tickets and reminded them of how essential it was that each person have one.

"Everybody good? Momma, you stand behind Julia. And Corrine, get in line behind Momma. Put Margot between you and Pete. We gone be alright, everybody!" Steddy carried Grate and held on to Julia's hand and led the way.

That is until Julia suddenly stopped walking.

"You alright, baby?" Steddy asked.

"Yeah…yeah. I'm fine. It's just-- no, I'll be alright." She rubbed her belly and released a long, deliberate breath.

As they drew closer to the ship, ushers wearing spacesuits herded them into a single file line that was one of fourteen other formed lines. A fleet of uniformed guards tossed passengers' luggage and belongings onto a conveyer belt so that it all could be checked for safety before being loaded onto the ship.

"Robots! Robots, daddy!" Grate pointed at the guards with joy.

Nervous excitement and the chatter of a thousand people sailed through the air. The entire scene felt like a dream as an eerie message repeated over loud speakers:

"Please form a single file line. Keep your ticket on your person at all times. Each passenger must have a ticket to board the shuttle. The Parlimont Family thanks you."

The fifteen neat lines led to the entrance ramp of the spaceship. They were organized by amusement park-styled dividing belts and directed to curve around like a maze. Dozens of armed guards stood at the top of the ramp as passengers were frisked and tickets were scanned. Behind the scanners were elevators that led to the lobby-level of the ship.

"It's a lot of people out here. Way more than I expected," Steddy whispered to Julia.

A woman's voice that shouted demands caught their attention. Then a she and a guard began to argue.

"What's happening? What's going on, Sted?" Julia nervously asked.

"I don't know. This lady's fussing at a guard at the entrance."

"Oh, no."

"Looks like folks are being turned away," Steddy said with concern.

"Turned away?" Julia gasped.

"Yeah. Aw, man... I think it's her parents!"

The lines of people watched as a weepy, elderly couple was being escorted away from the ship while their daughter continued to argue with the guard.

"They've forgotten their tickets! Can't you just confirm it with your bloody
system? Just look! Why won't you look?!"

"Rules are rules, Miss! It was made clear that each person had to have ticket in hand!" shouted the guard.

"Is this about money? Because I've got more money! Here, take it. Take everything!" She pulled out her wallet and check book.

The guard shook his head then noticed the attention of the crowd. "You're holding up the line. Either board the ship or join your parents. It's your choice!"

With that, the woman shoved the guard in the chest. "You're nothing but a bully! Let me speak with Parlimont!"

"Take her away!" commanded the guard.

"Wait! No! Let me see Parlimont! Let me speak with him! Do you know who I am?! You know who I am!" she yelled and kicked as two guards dragged her down the ramp and away from the spacecraft.

"They're taking her away, *too*!" Corrine exclaimed from behind Julia.

Grate clung to his father and hugged his neck. "Daddy, I'm scared," he whispered.

"You don't need to be afraid long as you're with me. You hear? Everything will be okay. I got you," Stedy assured his son. He then turned to his family. "Momma, you alright?"

"I'm making it. Be needing to sit soon," replied the Godmother.

"Just hold on a little while longer. How 'bout you, babe?"

"I'm fine," Julia answered as she continued to rub her belly.

"No need to panic, folks! Come on, keep coming! Keep walking this way. Have your tickets, chip-side up and ready to be scanned!" instructed the annoyed guard.

After a while, everything seemed to return to normal as passengers continued to board. That's when an attractive young man, who was famous for creating an online social network, that essentially ran itself and needed little input from the profile owner after a series of questions were answered. He was carrying a lap dog in an expensive bag and patting his jacket pockets in search of his ticket.

"No bags allowed, sir. You know the rules," the guard said with a chuckle. "And definitely no pets!"

"Victoria is *not* a pet! She's family! Don't you dare touch me," said the man to the guards as they reached for his bag. He then presented his tickets and waited.

"Look, I'm not going to do this with you, dude. Hand over the extra crap and be on your way."

"I bought *two* tickets, see? One for me and one for Victoria. Why would my assistant get her a ticket if she couldn't come to Bethiter?!"

"I don't know what this is about, but the rules were very, *very* clear. You have two options right now: come inside alone… or go back home with your little puppy and handbag."

The guards laughed amongst themselves.

"I'm sorry, I don't see what's funny. Is this somehow funny to you?" The man slung his blonde bang away from his face and tapped his foot.

"What's going on now?" Julia asked.

"Uh, seems this guy doesn't want to leave his dog. He's causing a scene."

"His dog?! Good grief! You can't be serious right now." She sucked air through her teeth and grabbed Steddy's arm.

"You alright?"

"I need to sit. I'm hurting," she said as she gave his arm a squeeze.

"Okay. Lean on me, baby. Come on. It won't be too much longer."

"DON'T TOUCH ME!" the man screamed at the guards. He exhaled then gently stroked the top of his Yorkie's head. "Do you have any idea who I am?" he asked.

"Ah, here we go again! We get it, we get it. You paid lots of money for this ticket. Well look around. Every single person in line did the same exact thing! Every person in that line is rich and famous and "important." But right now, *I'm* what stands in between life and death." The guard beat his chest with his fist. "*Me*! Do as I say or get out of my face!"

"Or what?" The man said as he reached into his bag and pulled out a revolver. He pointed it at the guard with shaking hands and stared directly into his eyes.

The surrounding guards immediately aimed their weapons back at him.

"Get down! Everybody down!" Steddy commanded as he helped Julia to the ground and covered Grate's body with his own.

"I would drop the weapon if I was you," the guard smugly gave. "It won't end well."

"Oh yeah?!" The man cocked his gun, but was instantly shot in the chest before he could blink.

Screaming was heard throughout the multitude of people as the man fell to the floor with his loyal companion by his side. A wailing alarm began to sound and bright, emergency lights flashed all around.

"Sted?!" cried Julia.

"Stay down!"

"Clean this up! Get him outta here!" spat the guard while stepping away momentarily to find a bullhorn. "Listen! Listen, everyone!" he hollered through the device. "I need you all to calm down and do as I say! Have your ticket ready! There *must* be a ticket for each, individual person! NO BAGS, NO ANIMALS, NO FOOD OR DRINKS!" He cursed under his breath and signaled for the alarms to be reset.

After the shock lifted, people returned to their orderly positions and cautiously approached the guards. People, who secretly didn't have tickets, quickly exited the lines while others tearfully released their dogs, cats, birds, and other animals that had been hidden away.

"Everybody alright?" Steddy asked as he stood. "Momma? Corrine? Pete? Margot?"

"Yeah, we're all fine. This is plum crazy! If this is how it starts...Lord!" The Godmother shook her head.

"Oh no..." Julia whimpered.

"What's wrong?" Steddy helped her stand.

"I think my water broke... Oh my God," she whispered.

"Grate, baby… let Auntie Corrine hold ya for a spell. Julia, you gotta stay calm. Hear me? Keep it together, Babygirl." The Godmother passed Grate to Corrine then began to rub Julia's lower back. "Shhhh… Shhhh…"

"Don't be scared, Gratey! You want some bubble gum?" Young Margot smiled at her cousin.

Steddy looked around. "Can you make it onto the ship, Babe?"

"She's gonna have to! What sort of question is that? Now shush! Everybody act normal. Let's go!" urged the Godmother. "She's fine, she's fine," she said to the rest of the family that peeked from behind.

Elevator doors slid open and out sprang Pastor Brooks. He wore a curious expression as he jogged to the ticket-scanning area. "What's going on out here?! I heard gunshots." He approached the guard that was holding the bullhorn. "Was anyone hurt?"

"Some thug was trying to sneak on the ship. He had a weapon. Everything is under control, Pastor," the guard answered.

"A thug? But…how?"

"Please return to your cabin, sir. It ain't safe for nice folks like you. People are animals during times like these, ya know."

The lines slowly moved forward. Julia hummed to distract herself and shifted her weight from one side to the other as the contractions worsened.

"No, no, no!" Godmother whispered to Julia, who'd started to hunch over. "You can't let them see you!"

"Momma, she's coming… I can't do this! I can't!"

"Yes, you can! Steddy, get her. Hold her up. We're almost there."

"I got you, baby. Just hold on." Steddy turned to face Julia and looked down at her wet feet.

"I should've worn pants. Oh my God!"

"No, honey you're fine. Come on, the line's moving."

Julia nodded but didn't move. "Let me go, Sted."

"What? Girl, come on."

"Let me *goooo*... ughhhhh!" Julia gave a low growl before crouching down like a quarterback preparing to receive the football from the center.

"Get up! Julia, up!" Steddy pulled at his wife until she was upright again. "You can't do this, baby. We're here. Get up! Please! Corrine, pass Grate up here to me."

"Okay," Julia sighed. She stood and wiped the sweat from beneath her nose.

"Mommy?! Is mommy having my sister?" Grate stared at his mother with concern.

"Look at how big the spaceship is, Gratey!" Steddy pointed. "What's the first thing you're gonna do when you get to Bethiter?"

Several minutes later, Julia reached behind her and tapped the Godmother. "Ughhhhhh, Ma!" She squatted once more.

"Move, Momma. Let me help her." Corrine slid in front of her mother and supported Julia by her elbows. "I got ya, sis. Keep breathing. You're doing good."

By this time, the Watters family was next in line. Steddy presented three tickets to the guard and smiled. Luckily, the guards had been so busy with the other passengers that no one noticed Julia's distress.

"Hello, sir. These are for me, my boy, and my wife."

"Alright. Ya'll step forward. Can he walk?"

"Yes."

"Put him down and let him walk then. Kids get patted down, too."

"Yes, sir. Also, my wife's visually impaired. Can I help her—"

"Step forward. You two can go to that guard over there. Security Station number three. I'll be sure to explain everything to your wife."

Steddy hesitated. "I'd be more comfortable if—"

"That way!" said the guard.

Steddy obeyed his instructions and proceeded to the next station. He handed the scanned tickets to a second guard, who lightly patted Grate's sides. Steddy anxiously watched as Julia's ticket was scanned and a female guard led her to a security station.

"My mommy's having a baby!" Grate announced proudly.

Steddy gulped.

"That's really cool, man! I bet you're gonna be a terrific big brother! Isn't that right?" The guard then stood tall and fixed his eyes on Steddy. "Hello, Mister Watters, sir. It's a pleasure to meet you! Believe it or not, but I wanted to be just like you when I was a little boy. Even got your number tattooed on my back. You're the best receiver of all time! Please raise your arms, sir."

Steddy looked over at Julia. The guard was patting her legs.

"Twenty-five seasons, almost 1,800 receptions, more than 200 touch downs," continued the young guard. "You're my hero, Mister Watters! I'm going to have to pat your crotch area now if that's okay..."

The guard, who was with Julia, noticed her wet face and knelt before her to perform a thorough inspection. The guard's gloved hand traveled underneath Julia's dress and near her inner thigh. After several seconds, the guard's eyes widened, and her face turned red. She then called for another female guard to join her and said something over her two-way radio. Julia looked horrified.

Steddy immediately took Grate by the hand and rushed to his wife. "Is everything alright?" he asked.

"Please return to your station, sir."

"This is my wife! What's the problem?"

"He's my husband. Please."

The two guards looked at each other.

The first guard stepped closer to him and whispered, "The head is out!"

"Are you serious?! She needs a doctor then! How you feeling, baby?"

Grate covered his ears with his hands and squeezed his eyes shut.

"Sir, please calm down and lower your voice."

"She needs medical attention and ya'll are just standing here, looking around!"

The guard removed her plastic gloves. "I'm sorry, sir but the issue is—"

"The issue is the newborn is considered another person... that needs a ticket," interrupted the guard with the bullhorn.

"Oh my God!" Hot tears began to roll down Julia's face.

"Nah! No. Wait a minute. Let me talk to your superior," demanded Steddy.

An urgent knock at Dr. Parlimont's door awoke Junior and Garla from their naps.

"Go back to sleep! Close your eyes, you two," he said.

The knocking continued.

"Oh, what is it?!" Parlimont shouted.

"It's Pastor Brooks! May I come in?"

"Oh. Yes, do come in!" he replied with a more chipper tone.

The pastor was sweaty and short of breath. "Pardon me, but I came here as fast as I could. You're needed outside."

"What's the matter? Have some water, Pastor."

"No, I don't want any water, Doctor P. There's a woman downstairs at security. She's having a baby. She has a ticket. But they won't let her board the ship. It's the craziest thing!"

"Oh," Parlimont rolled his chair to a side table and poured water into a glass. "The guards will handle it," he said as he offered the glass of water to Brooks.

"Hampton, please! It's a mess out there. She needs to be seen by a doctor. The guards *killed* a man earlier!"

Parlimont tried to hide his smile.

"I'm afraid for that poor woman! Please, Doc."

"Very well. Show me where she is."

The guards stood at attention once the elevator doors opened to reveal Dr. Parlimont. He beamed with pride and waved to them as he rode by. Pastor Brooks marched beside him and searched the stations for Julia.

"There she is!" he pointed. "That way!"

"Hey, Doctor Parlimont!" announced the excited guard, who couldn't seem to take his eyes off of Steddy. "Do you know who this is right here?! It's Steddy Watters, the greatest receiver in history!"

Parlimont frowned. He slowly approached the tall, muscular sports hero and his beautiful wife. "What seems to be the matter?"

"Oh, thank God! Thank you so much for coming out here, Doctor Parlimont. My wife is having our baby and *they* won't let her board the ship. Her ticket's been scanned and she's been patted down. The rest of our family has been cleared already and—"

"Tell you what, I'll make sure that Mrs…" Parlimont lazily pointed in Julia's direction.

"Watters, sir. Julia Watters."

"…Watters is taken care of so you can run along and join your family."

"What? No, I wanna stay with my wife."

Parlimont scowled and rolled his eyes.

Pastor Brooks rushed over to Steddy. "Mister Watters, I'm Pastor Brooks."

"I know who you are, Pastor."

"Bless you. I went to get Doctor P for ya'll. I promise to stay by her side." He shook Steddy's hand and whispered in his ear. "Things are getting sort of sticky out here. I think it's best you do what he asks. I'll make sure she's treated properly, sir. You have my word."

"Nah," Steddy shook his head.

"Sted, go! Go," Julia voiced. Her lips quivered.

Steddy marched to her and kissed her forehead as he held the sides of her face. "I love you, Babygirl. They're gonna take good care of you, alright?"

"I love you more. And tell Grate that I love him." Tears streamed from her eyes and nose and ran down her lips.

"Hey, hey… The two of you will be up there with us in no time. In no time. You hear me, Baby?"

Parlimont checked his watch and huffed. "Can one of you escort him to his suite?"

"I will!" blurted the star-struck guard from before. "Right this way, Mister Watters. I'll show you where to go! You can't tell by looking at me now, but I used to run a 100 in 11 seconds." The guard's banter echoed through the hall and could be heard until the elevator doors closed.

Parlimont scratched his chest over his shirt then summoned the guard with the bullhorn. "Russell, come over." He turned his chair so that his back was to everyone before he whispered to the senior security guard.

After a moment, the guard nodded and with a group of three others, escorted Julia down the ramp and around the ship. Pastor Brooks began to follow them.

"Uh, Pastor! A word please," announced Dr. Parlimont.

"Can it wait, Doc? I promised to stay with Missus Watters."

"No," chuckled Parlimont. "It cannot."

"But…" Pastor Brooks turned to see where they'd taken Julia.

Just then, a muscular guard stepped in front of Brooks to block his view. He tapped the rifle that hung from his shoulder. "Doctor Parlimont wants to speak with you," he huffed.

Pastor Brooks dropped his gaze. "Unbelievable," he said to himself before turning to Parlimont. "Yes, what did you want to talk about, Hampton?"

"With all due respect, I strongly advise that you keep out of matters that don't concern you, Pastor."

"Is that a threat?"

"Take it however you like." With that, Dr. Parlimont steered his chair toward the elevators and drove away.

"Where are they taking her? Will she be allowed to board?!" Brooks shouted. "I'm going to find her!"

Parlimont stopped his chair and frowned. "If that's what you want, then who am I to stop you?" he said without turning around.

Pastor Brooks ran his hands through his hair as Parlimont and his guards entered the elevator. He looked down at the mass of people waiting to get onto the ship and remembered his promise to Steddy. "Father, I need you," he prayed before leaving to find Julia.

"It's not easy being God," Parlimont said as the elevator doors closed.

The trip from Earth to Bethiter took more than a year. When the spacecraft took-off without Julia, Steddy nearly lost his mind. He'd been told that complications, which were beyond the medical knowledge of any doctor there, forced them to leave her behind. Steddy never received any answers to his many questions. He didn't know if Julia was alive or if his daughter had been safely delivered. He became quick-tempered and irrational. Thusly, the Godmother became Grate's guardian and did her best to protect him from Steddy's unpredictable coping mechanisms. Soon after takeoff, Steddy was placed in a solitary confinement of sorts due to his refusal to leave from outside Dr. Parlimont's suite.

Concerning the Brooks' family, Emersyn Brooks lived in a state of denial upon learning that her husband wasn't joining them on the new planet. She remained kind and cheerful and spoke of the pastor as if he were just in the next room. She'd be seen talking and laughing to herself or even attempting to pass her daughter, Serenity, to an invisible man. One ordinary evening during dinner, she pulled the knife from a turkey and climbed the table to attack Dr. Parlimont. As expected, the guards stopped her before she could cause any real damage. After that day, she was never seen or heard from again, although various rumors floated about for years.

Coincidentally, Dr. Hampton Parlimont, who preferred solitude and never considered fatherhood until meeting his wife, found himself parenting three children: Hampton Junior, Garla Lastoré, and Serenity Brooks.

Chapter Twenty-One: Parlimont Manor IV

"Look! There she is!" Ker cheered as Lucille Two descended from the sky.

The long-necked reptile swooped down and landed in the backyard of Parlimont Manor. Grate and Ker, while carrying Argan on his back, crept from the side of the house to meet her.

"Where's the strongwater?" Grate asked.

Lucille Two lowered her head and opened her large beak to reveal a clay jar with a lid.

"Perfect. Thank you, Jinxt." Grate took the jar and removed its lid as he quickly stepped to Argan, whose leg had been bleeding for hours.

Lucille Two frowned and transformed into an Argan replica. "Lucille Two," she insisted.

The foaming strongwater filled Argan's wound.

"What?" Grate asked.

"My name is Lucille Two. It is no longer Jinxt."

"Oh, I see." Ker nodded in agreement.

"How does it feel? Here, drink some as well." Grate brought the jar to Argan's lips.

"You are odd, King Grate," stated Lucille Two.

"Huh?" Grate looked at her briefly then shook his head. "How does it feel, Argan? Try to stand."

"You value my shifting ability and the ways in which I assist you, but I wonder if you truly value me."

Ker and Argan stared at the ground. Grate took a deep breath and approached the shifter.

"I am truly sorry. I value *and* appreciate you. Beyond your capabilities and what you do for me. *All* parts of you."

"Then I expect to be called Lucille Two."

"Yes. I will do my best. You have my word, Lucille Two."

Argan laughed to herself and winked at Lucille Two.

Once Argan's leg was fully healed, the crew snuck to the rear of the manor. They peered through the windows and noticed most of the lights were off or dimmed.

"I don't see anyone," whispered Grate. "They must all be in bed." He then turned to Lucille Two and hesitated. "How is my Grandmother?"

"She is well and sleeping."

"And what of the girl? Lucille."

"She worries about her mother. Margot is her name. The elders are looking after her and tending to the infant humans."

Grate nodded. "Thank you. I'm relieved." He wished he'd acted sooner when his cousin had first warned him about Dr. Robot's plans. He gripped the window sill with his fingertips and searched the Parlimont kitchen with his eyes. He wondered if his father would attempt to fight him… or if he'd recognize him at all.

"Grate," Argan gently voiced as she touched his shoulder. "We cannot wait here forever."

"Right. I'll break through the back door. Stay close to me. Lucille Two, follow Argan. Ker, protect from behind."

"Yes, Your Majesty! I will not let you down!" Ker assured.

"Shhhh!" Argan urged. "Do you wish to let everyone know that we are here?"

"Oh. I am sorry," said Ker.

"It is alright," smiled Lucille Two.

"Listen," warned Grate with intensity. "We will only fight if provoked. Is that understood?"

Everyone agreed.

The king stayed low and quickly used the tip of his knife to pry open the door. The four of them entered and were stunned by the stillness of the home.

Crunch!

Argan and Grate turned to find Lucille Two enjoying a crisp apple that she'd found on the counter. Ker licked his lips as his stomach grumbled.

"Shhh! You must behave," Argan urged. She snatched the apple from her clone and returned it to the countertop.

The four circled around the spacious kitchen, peeked into the dining area, and then headed for a hallway that lead to countless rooms.

"Something is not right here," whispered Lucille Two.

Grate kept his back against the wall as he turned the doorknobs of one of the chambers and pushed it open. They looked around, but found no one inside. Grate, who'd become green with worry, perked up as he thought he heard a baby's cry.

"Do you hear that? Do you hear crying?" he asked.

Ker cocked his head to the side and stared at the ceiling. Lucille Two shrugged her shoulders. Argan shook her head and proceeded toward the hallway.

"No," she answered. "Please let me lead, my king."

After finding a study, a closet, a bathroom, and two more bedrooms… all empty… the foursome began to speed up their pace. Argan glanced into another bedroom that had no one inside.

"Should we climb upward? Did you bring the rope?" she asked.

"We won't need any rope. There will be stairs- a path that leads us to the next floor," Grate responded as he took a double take of the bedroom that Argan had just passed. His lips parted and he squinted at a framed picture that rested on a nightstand.

"King?" Ker said as he looked around.

Without a thought, Grate turned on the lamp that sat next to the picture and stooped down to get a better view. It was an old photo of his mother! He fell to his knees as a myriad of emotions overcame him all at once. His stomach clenched and felt as though hundreds of tiny shooting stars were flying around.

Lucille Two entered the room and smiled at the woman in the picture. "Hello," she waved.

"What is that?" Argan asked as she and Ker stood around in awe of the miniature image.

"A photograph," he said as he fought back tears. "An image from the Old World… of my mother."

"What? She is beautiful!" Ker exclaimed.

"You have her face," added Argan.

"Where is she now?" asked Lucille Two.

Argan nudged her. Still holding the frame, Grate stood upright and sniffled as he looked around the peaceful room. A cup of half-finished tea rested on the nightstand beside a pair of reading glasses and can of black shoe polish. The bed was unmade. Three pairs of black dress shoes were lined up against the wall. Grate opened the closet doors to reveal a row of white, collared shirts, which were all neatly pressed. A half dozen black business suits were also hanging there. He searched the room with his eyes to find a woven basket of soiled clothes in the far corner. He rushed to the basket and pulled out a shirt then burrowed his face into it. His body trembled as he began to sob.

"What is happening?" Ker whispered to Argan.

She held up her hand, instructing him to be quiet. Grate wiped his face and mouth with the shirt before dropping it to the floor. He then removed the picture from the frame and slid it into his satchel. He looked at his three companions and bowed his head.

"Follow me." Grate marched into the hallway in search of the staircase.

"Wait," commanded Lucille Two. She stood at the doorway of the last bedroom.

"It's empty, we are going upstairs," said Grate.

"It is not empty," Lucille Two blinked.

Argan braced herself for battle. Ker's tail began to glow. Grate quickly slid across the wall and peered into the dim, modest room. Yet, he saw no one.

Lucille Two calmly went inside and pointed toward the backside of the door. "There."

Grate and Argan followed her and were stunned to find Garla hanging from the door by strips of curtains that had been tied around her neck. Lucille Two grabbed one her dangling hands as she transformed into a Garla look-alike.

"She is cold," Lucille Two remarked.

Grate used his knife to cut the curtain as Argan took hold of the body. She gently placed Garla onto the bed and searched for any signs of life but found none.

"Excuse me... Is this the Robot's doing?" Ker whispered from the doorway.

"I don't believe so," answered Grate.

"Do you understand these symbols, King Grate?" asked Lucille Two. She was holding a note that she'd retrieved from the nightstand.

Grate nodded and took the tear-stained paper. "Please find an alternate form, my friend."

Lucille Two shrugged; then shifted back into the Argan double. Grate read aloud.

To Whomever Finds Me:

I no longer have reason to stay. The cycle of boredom, jealously, and a loveless life eats at the spirit after a while. And I am tired of it all. I wish that I'd died alongside my mother; for, she is the only one who every truly loved me.

And to Dr. Parlimont... Hell is too good of a place for a rare evil such as yours.

With no regrets,
Garla A. Lastoré

"Follow me!" Grate huffed as he dropped the note and rushed out of the room. He curved around the corner, almost slipped, and found himself between two winding staircases and beneath an exquisite crystal chandelier. He looked down and saw his reflection in the shiny marble floor. His home in the Old World had floors like those. He swallowed hard to relieve his dry throat.

"Wow!" Exclaimed Ker upon seeing the chandelier. "It is like a cluster of fire fairies!"

"This is nauseating," Argan said with crossed arms. "Is this how the wealthy humans live? While we suffer and fear being killed when merely searching for food?"

"They appear to overindulge any time that they can," added Lucille Two.

"Do you come here often?" Ker asked her.

"I go many places. I see no purpose in being still."

Memories of hot Georgia summers and the taste of his mother's baked macaroni and cheese slipped away... returning to a secret nook in Grate's mind. "Come on! Stop wasting time!" he urged as he raced up the stairs.

Once they reached the top, Argan noticed a small, yellow blanket on the floor in front of a large half-opened door. Grate stopped to pick up the blanket while Argan approached the doors and listened for anything. With a quick nod, she signaled for them to follow her inside. And as with all of the other areas, the nursery was vacant.

"No one is here. The entire place is empty," Argan concluded as they returned to outside of the nursery.

"Where else could they be?" Ker admired a large portrait of Hampton and Serenity that hung on the wall in the hallway. "This human is lovely... like King Grate's mother!"

Argan rolled her eyes. "She is average really. They all look alike to me-- I mean, not the king's mother. But..."

"There, there," whispered Lucille Two as she rubbed Argan's back. "It is alright. King Grate did not hear you."

Embarrassed, Argan attempted to smile at Lucille Two until she noticed that he was gone. "King?" Argan moved away from the painting. "King Grate?"

"In here!" he called from another room.

"You two stay here in case anyone comes." Argan jogged through the next wing to find Grate in Hampton' office, thumbing through Dr. Parlimont's journals.

He'd been reading some of the "laws" that Parlimont passed such as no adopting children or marrying outside of one's class. And there was the one forbidding any discussion of what happened on the spaceship during the year-long trip to Bethiter. Grate scoffed, then picked up another journal to find the blueprint of the spacecraft and a map of all of the regions on Bethiter. It even included Parlimont's laboratory, which strangely, was located in The Stretch. He quickly tore out the pages and added them to his satchel.

"What is that?" Argan asked.

"Books of the Robot… his ideas… his dreams…the map to his lab… There are even drawings—" Grate stopped and slammed the book shut. "Let's go."

"Drawings of what?"

"I have the map of the lab. Come on." He proceeded toward the door.

"I want to see them."

"There is nothing to see. Let us go."

"Give me a moment. It is rather tempting," she said as she reached for journal.

"Argan, no. I don't think that you should."

Upon flipping it open, Argan found images of Parlimont's experiments involving the Surges and other native creatures. At first, he'd hoped that he could use *their* hearts to save the lives of the wealthy babies. He'd performed hundreds of transplant surgeries using Surge organs and monkeys but was unsuccessful each time. He'd also tried to make suits of armor made of Surge skin but found that its elasticity and impenetrable qualities were lost post-mortem. He'd dissected their bodies and committed other unimaginable crimes against Surges even while they were still living and awake. There was also a section dedicated to the various types of medicine and elixirs that he'd tried to make with their blood. Argan closed the book and looked down at the small tower of journals that rested on the desk.

Grate dropped his head, unsure of what to say. "I didn't want you to see that," he offered. He approached her with open arms in an attempt to embrace her, but she refused and threw him off of her. Grate flew back and collided with the bookshelves behind him.

Argan hissed and used her mighty wave to destroy everything in sight. Books flew from their shelves and trophies came crashing down to the floor. She sent a crystal decanter and glass set whizzing across the room and with a final thrust flipped the heavy desk over. Her fiery red eyes fixed on Grate as she showed her teeth.

"Argan??" He looked up at her from the floor.

Just then, Ker and Lucille Two appeared in the doorway.

"What a mess!" Ker announced.

Lucille Two grabbed one of Hampton's cigars from the floor and took a bite. "Humans are strange," she said before offering the rest of the cigar to Ker.

"I must get out of here!" Argan said as she ran from the room and out the front door.

Moments later, the trio discovered her vomiting in the backyard bushes.

"I, too, found the human domain rather sickening," Ker whispered to Grate.

Lucille Two approached her and presented the cigar. "Have some? It is not very good."

"No, thank you. Toss it." Argan glanced at Grate and looked away. "I am sorry. Please forgive—" she started.

"There's no need for you to apologize. Are you alright?" His gentle eyes smiled at her.

"Who knows?" she shrugged.

Grate walked over to Argan and kissed her forehead. Then he retrieved the map of the planet and blueprint of the lab from his bag and studied them. He'd never traveled to that part of Bethiter and knew that they'd need reinforcement. He quickly sketched a copy of both pages and drew an arrow highlighting the lab.

"Lucille Two, are you able to use this weapon?" He pointed to the axe on his hip.

"No."

"How about this one?" He pointed to his morning star on the other.

"No."

"Then you shouldn't come, it's too dangerous."

"Existence as the powerless has proven to be a war of its own. I will fight with you, King Grate!" Lucille Two appeared as a small cyclone and then took on Grate's image. She giggled.

Grate smiled at the shifter and sighed. "I prefer that you stay out of harm's way. But if you insist on joining us, please stay close to me at all times," he said. Next, he tied the pages that he was holding around the sea swallow's tail "Hyaaah!" he voiced as he slapped the backside of the sea swallow. It took off gliding toward the Onyx Caves alone. "It's late and we have darkness on our side," Grate figured. "We should keep going and not wait for the warriors. I believe that the Robot has taken everyone to his laboratory and my spirit weeps at the thought of what he may do."

The four huddled together while Grate shared his plan. Afterward, Lucille Two assumed the appearance of the giant, winged reptile once again so that the other three could ride her ridged back to the lab.

"Um…" Ker cleared his throat loudly.

"Is something wrong?" asked Grate.

"I'd rather not ride, Your Majesty," Ker mumbled.

"That's ludicrous! It would take you a day by land. Come!" Grate ordered as he and Argan climbed Lucille Two's dark, fleshy wings.

"No, no…"

"What is the matter, Ker?" Argan asked.

"It is just that… um…"

"Are you afraid of the open sky?"

Ker nodded and stared at the ground in shame. Argan hopped down from Lucille Two's back and met the eel.

"Do not be afraid. The open sky is foreign to me, too. We were not created for this predicament, yet we survive in spite of it. You are a deadly, electric warrior, who I am sure can swim at speeds faster than light!"

Ker chuckled and showed hundreds of jagged, clear teeth.

"It is not your fault that the barrier separates you from your natural habitat. And it is not your fault that you fear the open air. We are your friends and will be right beside you. Now, come on." Argan gave his lower neck a light punch and jogged back to Lucille Two.

Ker took a deep breath and looked toward the sky. "Here I come!"

Grate straddled Lucille Two and held onto one of the large ridges on her back. Argan sat behind him and wrapped her arms around his midsection while Ker sat on Lucille Two's rump and wrapped his tail around hers for extra security.

"Whoa, whoa, whoa, weeeeeeeeeeeeeeeeeeeee!" Ker yelled out with excitement as Lucille Two rocketed through the dazzling, black sky.

Chapter Twenty-Two: Parlimont Laboratory

"There!" Grate said to Lucille Two. "Land there, behind the hill!"

She nodded, then slowed to land behind a mound of dried-up coral reef. The human, Surge, and eel hopped down from her back, then she shifted into an Argan double once again.

"I am flattered," Argan voiced.

Lucille Two smiled. Grate peeked around the bulky reef, then referred to his map of the planet. "This is odd. According to his layout, the lab should be right over there, beside the lake."

"Let me see, King Grate," requested Ker, who was still giddy from overcoming his fear of heights. "Ah, yes. Yes. It should be right over there. The king is right!"

"Perhaps the map is incorrect," Argan suggested.

"No, that would be unusual. The Robot is precise and intentional." Grate scooped a handful of mud from the ground and smeared it across his arms, legs, and face. "Do you suppose that it's underground, Argan?"

"No. The pools would not allow that. They barely tolerate the humans above-ground."

"*Barely*," added Lucille Two.

"I see." Grate studied the map once more.

"Or maybe it is there, but… hidden," said Ker. He closed his eyes and became still. "I am sensing strong energy coming from that direction."

"Splendid. Lead the way," urged the king.

Just as Ker was about to leave the reef, they heard voices.

"Down! Everyone down!" whispered Grate.

The group peered around the mound and saw two guards, smoking in the distance. "That *must* be it!" he concluded.

"Ker, come with me. I will disarm them while you locate the entrance," said Argan. She looked at Grate for approval, then sprinted on all fours toward the guards.

The men were too preoccupied with their conversation to notice her. She quickly rose behind the first guard and broke his neck by grabbing his head and yanking it to the side. Then she struck the second in the chest so hard that his lungs collapsed. She stood over both bodies and admired her work while Ker inspected the area. His tail began to glow as he closed his eyes. Grate and Lucille Two quickly joined them.

"A blockage is here. Stand back," Ker told them. His entire body pulsated and his skin rippled. He reared his now sparking tail back and swung it over his head, which caused silver, electric waves to fling in front of him.

The tremoring waves clung to a vast invisible wall and connected to form a web, as far as the eye could see. After a moment, Argan then waved her arm in the web's direction, causing it to bend inward as if something being caught by a net. Seconds later, the web faded away, as did the simulated image of The Stretch. The four were now standing before a gray, single-story, U-shaped building. However, the U was squared and not curved. The Parlimont spacecraft rested behind in the distance, and the sight sent a chill down Grate's spine.

Lucille Two bent down to examine the guard with the broken neck. She touched his still-warm skin and caressed his curly, brown hair. Her green and black flesh turned peach colored as she adopted the guard's image. She picked up his heavy rifle and placed its strap over her shoulder.

"Good thinking!" said Argan. "Lead the way and distract the guards!"

"Be careful with that," Grate warned. He quickly slid the lanyards from around the guards' neck, which were clipped onto entry cards, but stopped upon noticing that one was wearing a golden necklace oddly similar to Margot's.

"Thank you, King Grate," Lucille Two whispered while reaching for a lanyard.

Grate placed it around her neck and used the other entry card to open the door. Lucille Two was excited to be involved and stood tall as she marched into the building. The remaining three peeked through the front door's window as the shape-shifter was stopped by one of the guards.

"Hey, is everything alright, Tim?" asked the guard.

"Why, yes. I wanted to come inside," Lucille Two replied. She continued to walk ahead until the guard turned around to face her and his back was to the front door.

"Things have escalated and it's important that every man be in place. Get back out there with Leonard!"

Another guard walked into the hallway from a side room, wearing only a t-shirt and boxers, and proceeded to a room at the far end of the hall. Moments later, a second guard exited the same room, holding a toothbrush and toothpaste. It seemed that these were the residential quarters for the guards. Grate carefully opened the front door and held it open as Ker and Argan snuck in and veered to the right. A lanky guard, who was manning that hallway was facing away from them, but preparing to turn around to walk in the opposite direction. Without hesitation, Argan fell to her hands and bolted toward the guard. The guard's blue eyes stretched wide as she started to scream for help, but it was too late. Argan waved in her direction before she could make a sound—which caused her to lose consciousness—and caught her before she collapsed onto the tile. The Surge then punched her with only a portion of her strength and smashed her face in as if it were a piece of fruit. Argan batted her bright, amber eyes and quickly dragged the body to her partners. Ker's bottom jaw dropped in amazement.

"This way!" Grate mouthed as he pointed toward a door to his left and charged in. It was mostly dark inside and filled with long tables, with chairs stacked on top. Besides a few refrigerators, sinks, and a couple of ice machines, the room wasn't much to behold. The three quickly scanned the dining hall but found no one there. Argan slung the guard's body to the side and suggested they separate.

Ker dashed into the room across from them. And it was empty. Argan hurried to the room next to that one and it was empty as well. Grate started to enter the room next to the dining area, but it was just a utility closet. All three peeked from their respective places and returned to the hallway. They checked each room, one by one, but came out with nothing helpful and no one of interest. Finally, they reached the last door of the perpendicular hallway and stumbled upon two guards getting frisky in the study lounge of a small library.

"Put your hands in the air and don't make a sound!" commanded Grate, with his battle axe extended.

The unnerved guards did as they were told, although the man appeared to be only seconds away from fainting while the woman seemed more insulted by the intrusion.

"Where is the laboratory?!" Grate spat.

"That way! Puh-Puh-Please let me live!" Cried the guard.

His partner rolled her eyes. Argan smirked and stepped to her, leaving only an inch between them. "I do not like your spirit," she said before grabbing the guard by the throat and lifting her into the air. "Humble yourself or perish. Am I understood?"

The guard kicked her legs in erratic motions and scratched at the hand that was wrapped around her neck. Tears gathered in the outside corners of her eyes as her face turned purplish-red. Bubbles of salvia burst across her puckered lips. Calmly, Argan returned the guard to the floor and released her. The woman gasped for air and fell to her knees.

"Show us the way to the lab," Grate said to the male guard.

"But—" the guard blurted. He looked down at his lover, who was still recuperating on the floor.

"Go!" Grate commanded.

"Rise to your feet. Come," growled Argan to the guard that she'd choked.

The shaky guard led them down the third hall and up to large metal, double doors. He explained that Dr. Parlimont's suite was at the end of the hallway and that no additional guards were to be expected as it was *his* night to protect that zone. He stopped in front of the doors and stared blankly at the king.

"Go on!" urged Grate.

"Uh… is it… I need to… can I—"

"Oh, for the love of the sphere! He needs to use his badge to open the stupid door!" his companion said.

By that time, Argan, who'd missed the smell of human fear and grown tired of the woman's sour attitude, turned to her then shoved her fist straight through her belly. A gruesome expression struck the woman's face. She let out a little squeak as drool fell from her open mouth. Her bloodshot red eyes, fixed on her lover, rolled to the back of her skull. She collapsed onto the floor once Argan retracted her arm.

"Well, use your badge then!" said Argan, flinging her hand. Tiny chunks of flesh and blood splattered across the tile.

The unstable guard, who watched in horror, wobbled from side to side briefly before fainting. Grate jumped behind to catch him then used his badge to unlock the electronic door. The light on the lab door turned from red to green and a faint beeping sound was heard as the doors slid open.

"Grab her and come on," grunted Grate as he followed Ker into the lab. The blacked-out guard was heavier than he looked.

"Oh, what difference does it make?" Argan whispered. She looked down at the bloody mess and wondered from where humans garnered their copious pride.

"Woweeeee!" Ker whispered at the sight of the research facility.

"Mother Infinity be my guide!" Argan gave while dragging the guard's lifeless body behind her.

Grate placed the unconscious guard on the floor and stared around him in amazement. The laboratory was filled with impressive instruments for scientific experiments and a number of telescopes, in several sizes, with various sensitivities. Flasks and beakers that held liquids of all colors rested on tables. Lab coats, aprons, and protective eyewear hung along the walls. The humming of aquarium filters could be heard as there were several tanks that housed captured Bethiter water creatures. There were maps of the other nine new worlds and an image of Bethiter that was photographed from outer space. There was also a large map of the solar system. And next to the map was a sketch of the changes that the solar system had undergone over the past twenty-three years.

Just as they were about to walk into the next room, something caught Grate's eye. "Hold on," he said to himself as he returned to the map of the solar system.

"What is it?" Argan asked. "Keep a look out, Ker," she said as she rushed to the king.

Grate looked over to the map, and then back at Dr. Parlilmont's sketch of the changes. He studied the sketch, and then ran his finger along the solar system map. His mouth went dry as he hurried to one of the telescopes and turned it toward the large glass window. He peered into the eyepiece then quickly referred to the solar system map and then focused the scope.

"Grate?" Argan nervously said.

He slowly turned to her, with a look of defeat and horror. "Everything I've been told is a lie."

**Chapter Twenty-Three: Parlimont
Laboratory II**

On the other side of the building, Lucille Two was still in disguise and had been keeping up with the guard as he patrolled the hall. She smiled and waved at another guard, who was exiting the shower room and replied with a curious look as he returned to his bunk. The shifter shrugged then watched the hall monitor blow his nose into a piece of tissue. She admired his broad chest and unusually large ear lobes. For a moment she considered changing her appearance to match that of his. But then she realized that doing so may not be the best thing to do.

The guard took a double take at Lucille Two and frowned. "What are you looking at, man?"

"Your ears."

He stopped walking. "What in the sphere is up with you, Tim?"

"Nothing."

"Get back out there to your post and quit fooling around! Or I'll have to report you," he warned.

"Where are the hostages?"

"What?" gulped the guard.

"I would like to do some testing. Like the ones you did with Argan's brother. Please show me the way."

"Huh? Argan?" The guard reached for his pistol that rested on his hip.

"The tests that Doctor Robot conducts, I am interested in those," she kindly stated.

"Doctor Robot?!" With that, he drew his weapon.

Lucille Two gasped and shifted into a fire fairy. The guard immediately pulled the trigger at the sight. The fairy fluttered in circles for a while, dodging the bullets, before zooming down the hall and around the corner. The frantic guard ran to a glass box on the wall and punched through it to press a large red button in the middle. Blinding lights began to flash and blaring sirens could be heard throughout the building. Sleeping guards sprang from their beds and dressed in their gear.

"Oh, no!" Ker yelled through the wailing siren.

"Grate, what should we do? Grate!" Argan shouted.

He didn't move. He stood there with his eyes fixed on the sketch of the only unnamed planet on the map… Earth. Memories of playing little league baseball with his parents cheering him on from the stands flooded his mind. He remembered painting his little sister's nursey pink and being ecstatic about the new addition to the family. Then he thought of how afraid his mother looked while they stood in line to board the spacecraft… how she couldn't stop her tears from falling but managed to smile at him each time she heard his voice.

The guard, who laid on the floor at Grate's feet was roused by the excitement. He opened his eyes and looked around. After realizing that no one was paying him any attention, he quickly sprang to his feet and ran towards the exit.

"Not so fast," Ker said as he blocked the doors.

"King Grate! Come!" Argan urged with a gentle wave that pushed Grate to the side. "And you," she turned to the guard. "Take us to the Robot! Now!"

"Who?!"

"Your leader!"

"I will clear the way!" Ker yelled. He zapped the double doors' access pad with his charged, electric tail, and caused them to fly open. The moment he exited the lab, a fleet of armed guards rushed from the right. Ker showed his rows of barbed, clear teeth and roared. Two of the guards took off running in the other direction at the sight. Ker slung his tail their way and it cracked like a whip. Shards of electric bolts struck the group of guards. Several electrocuted bodies lost control and began to seize across the floor. Unaffected soldiers stumbled over their peers while they took aim and shot at the giant eel. Ker grunted as the bullets penetrated his translucent skin. Bright, blue electric waves zapped at each entry point. He closed his eyes tightly and pulled his head and neck down into his body like a turtle. The guards continued to shoot. Ker's body started to rumble. His skin rippled and the glow from his tail spread over every part of his massive frame. His trembling sped up when suddenly, two heads broke through his neck and a second tail sprang from the first. The guards continued to shoot, but the fortified eel now had twice the amount of strength and fury. Both heads released a ferocious battle cry of rage. The tails tremored and shone brighter than ever before.

The pitiful guard led Argan and Grate to the connecting room next to the laboratory. Here, there were shelves stocked with surgical instruments, extra lab equipment, and specimen jars. Argan and the king gawked at one another as they quickly passed hundreds of jars filled with preserving fluid and various organs, unborn animals, and deceased babies… mostly from The Community. One might've questioned the origin of the babies had not the shelf been labeled "Community Spoil." There was a wall with outstretched animal hide and eel skin. Several gigantic Surge tails hung from the ceiling as trophies.

"This way," said the guard. He pointed to a door that opened to the hallway.

"Continue!" Argan snapped. "You will take heed where your feet go. Death for us means death for you!"

The flashing lights allowed Lucille Two to fly above the battling guards and eel without being noticed. She stayed close to the ceiling and went from door to door until she discovered one with a large vent opening at the top. She entered the room and found two men being held hostage: James and Ben, the bodyguards from Parlimont Manor. The men sat on the floor, tied together by rope. They were both severely beaten, and Ben was unconscious. Also, his right eye was covered by a bandage. A spot of blood was seeping through it.

Lucille Two lowered to the floor and assumed human form, as not to alarm them. "Hello," she said with a wave and a smile.

James stared at her in shock. "Lucille?! How'd you get in here?"

"I am not Lucille. I am Lucille Two."

"Huh? Are you one of Doctor Parlimont's experiments?"

"No."

He lifted his head and stared suspiciously. "How do you know Lucille then?"

"Lucille, the human girl, is my friend. Is she your friend, too?"

"Is she hurt?! Where is she?"

"No. She is in the caves."

"But how- no never mind. Hey, can you untie us?"

"Yes." Lucille Two blinked.

"Is something wrong?"

"Yes, many things are wrong. Is that your friend as well?" She pointed to Ben.

James nodded. Gunshots continued outside in the halls.

"Please untie us!"

"Alright. I will."

Grate and Argan followed the guard to the end of the long hallway. They ducked and moved as quickly as possible while Ker fought the last of the soldiers at the other end. The flashing red and yellow lights combined with the obnoxious siren made the battle scene appear choppy and unreal. The eel seemed to move in slow motion as he shot bolts of lightning from his tail and snatched guards off of their feet by his mouth.

"This is his bedroom!" yelled the guard with his hands cupped over his ears. Argan motioned for him to proceed.

"Do I have to?!"

"Yes!" boomed Grate as he lifted his battle axe.

The guard whimpered before unwillingly opening the door and immediately threw his hands in the air. "I am being held hostage! They killed Melanie! Please help me!" he sobbed.

Argan rolled her eyes. Grate closed the door behind him. Russell, Dr. Parlimont's senior security guard, was sitting in the middle of the room with a pistol on his lap and his swollen leg securely wrapped and propped up on a chair. Hampton was also there with his back to them. He sat in his father's electric wheelchair, facing his father, who was asleep in a dated hospital bed. The old man wore an oxygen mask and had an IV drip connected to his arm. A bandage covered his blind eye. He'd apparently undergone an operation during that short time. The room was plain and small. There was only an old desk covered with papers and a bedside commode. Russell released a long sigh before reaching over to tap Hampton on the shoulder. Hampton hiccupped then slowly turned around. He held a glass of dark liquor and was obviously inebriated. His eyes widened with a twisted sense of pleasure as he eyed Grate.

He took a sip of his drink and started to speak; but then pointed to his ear and held up his finger for them to wait.

"One moment," he mouthed with a relaxed smile. He walked in one direction and then stopped to go in the other. Finally, he ended at the wall beside his father's desk and flipped a switch that caused the sirens and flashing lights to cease.

"Much better! Am I right?" he said, making a toasting gesture.

"Mister Parlimont, sir! Please! I've been held against my will and I'm so sorry for leading them here, but I had no other choice and I'm honestly unsure of how many of our men are gone! There's another creature with them—"

"Stop," said Hampton. "What's your name?"

"Um, Brent, sir," answered the guard as he slowly relaxed his arms.

"Russell, shoot Brent."

"No!" cried the guard as Russell pointed his gun and pulled the trigger. Brent crashed to his knees, and then fell to the side.

Hampton wiggled his index finger in his ear and scrunched his face. "My ears are still ringing! He was annoying, right?"

Russell laughed to himself.

Hampton took another sip from his drink and pointed toward his father. "He… is dying. The old fool performed surgery on himself because he wanted a new… eye. Comatose," he burped.

Argan looked at Grate, moving only her eyes. He responded with subtle approval. In the same instance she waved her arm in Russell's direction, causing his pistol to blow across the room. She immediately raced to him, caught him by the neck, and slammed him into the cement wall behind him. Blood trickled from his nose as she released him. She blinked her bright, crimson eyes and turned to find Hampton pointing a hand-held laser at Grate.

"Do you like it? One of father's inventions," he asked.

"Yargh!" she bellowed with a mighty wave of her arm. Within a fraction of a second, she was hurled back against the wall and sliding to the floor.

Hampton stared at her, unfazed. Grate stepped toward her.

"Not another step," warned Hampton.

Argan shook her head and gathered her composure as she returned to her feet. She looked at Grate with horror hanging from her face. Grate stared back, confused. Hampton's eyes bounced from her to Grate and then back at her.

"Oh!" he chuckled. He held up his finger, as if to tell them to wait, with the hand that held his glass and finished the drink with several gulps. Although his sobriety level was questionable, he faithfully kept Grate as his target with the laser gun. After placing the glass upon the desk, he loosened his tie and pulled down the side of his shirt collar to reveal a silver ring around his neck. It was about an inch wide and had several buttons along the front. "Another one of father's inventions," he proudly announced while tapping the metal ring.

Argan fixed her eyes on Dr. Parlimont.

"Father wears one too. He warned me about the lizard people with special abilities. You will have no luck here, monster. It also makes your little tricky moves ineffective on us." He eyed Russell's body and snarled. "Try anything like *that* again and I'll kill you both!" Hampton then turned to the king. "Grate, we finally meet. And damn, you're a big one! I wish father could see you. Your heart's probably worth more than I am!" He stared at Grate for a moment. "Place your weapons on the floor. One by one."

Grate tightened his grip on his battle axe.

"NOW!"

"Alright... placing..." He laid the axe on the floor in front of him, and did the same with his flail.

"Slide them this way with your foot... Good." Hampton kicked both pieces underneath his father's bed and released a sigh of relief. "You might be glad to know that Russell killed Margot."

Grate's eyes widened. Argan growled.

"Wait, no, I said that incorrectly." He quickly shook his head and held the bridge of his nose for a moment. "Okay. You might be glad to have Russell dead because Russell killed Margot." Hampton bit his bottom lip as he watched the king's brow furrow. "Karma, right? ...Or is it justice?"

"Where is everyone?" asked Grate.

"Everyone like who?"

"My father." He nearly choked on the words. He hadn't said them in more than a decade.

Hampton belched again and rubbed his chest. "Excuse me. That was rude... follow me." He walked backwards, still pointing the gun.

They followed him out of the bedroom's side door, which led outside and to the spacecraft. A mosaic of colorful emotions came over Grate. Then he remembered seeing his former planet intact.

They followed Hampton on-board the ship.

"Remember this?" he cheerfully asked. "I do!" He took a deep breath of satisfaction. "Just look at how well-preserved father has kept it!" He knocked on the outside of the ship. "...like new!"

"*Where* is my father?" growled the king.

"Hey, hey, in due time. Enjoy the tour. Father's guards are all a bunch of "yes men" so it is nice to have you here. I mean that."

After a senseless walk through the spaceship and a moment of watching Hampton relieve himself in the restroom, they finally reached the front of the ship.

"Here we are...The flight deck! Go on in!"

The space was large enough for a dozen people. Once Grate and Argan were inside, Hampton passed them and proceeded across the room to the flight controls, while walking backwards again and aiming at the two. He stopped walking when he reached the pilot and copilot chairs. "It's been a while since you've seen your father, no?"

Grate's nervous belly clenched into a hard knot. Argan gritted her teeth and considered attacking. Hampton grabbed the pilot chair by its headrest and spun it around to display Steddy, with duct tape over his mouth and rope tied around his wrists and legs.

"Surprise!" Hampton straightened Steddy's collar and brushed imaginary lint off his shoulder.

"You son of a black hole," Grate fumed.

Argan's eyes glowed the reddest red.

"What's it been, Steven? Ten... twenty years?" Hampton asked as he tapped Steddy's shoulder with the barrel of the laser gun.

Steddy stared into Grate's eyes and remained calm.

"Here we are! One big happy family!" Hampton chuckled. "Oh! Speaking of family... Pardon me for a minute. I'd like for you to meet *my* family." He made Steddy the target of his aim then backed away toward the cabin's closet. He opened it to reveal Sara, sitting on the floor with the baby in her arms. She was still wearing her nightgown and bathrobe. Duct tape covered her mouth and her wrists were tied together in front of her.

"Grate, this is my family! My wife, Sara and…" he trailed off. "I'm ashamed to say that in the midst of all of this… excitement, this little sweetie has yet to be named." Hampton pulled Sara by the elbow as he stomped over to Steddy. "Can you think of a name, Steven?!" He pointed the gun at Sara's head and pressed his nose against Steddy's cheek.

Sara stared at the floor and stiffened. She snorted and jerked in terror.

"I looked up to you as a father! I respected you! I loved you, Steddy!" Hampton stepped away from the old man and wiped his face. "…More than I loved anyone! And you betray me?" He grieved with a look of disgust.

A confused Grate and Argan glanced at each other. Grate slowly shook his head as to urge her not to strike.

"THIS CHILD IS NOT MINE!" Hampton boomed while jabbing the laser gun in the air toward Sara's head. A string of saliva fell from his bottom lip.

Sara shut her eyes tightly and her muffled crying became louder. Her bright red face began to perspire as she cradled the baby close to her chest.

"Grate, it saddens me to report that your father and *my* wife have been having an affair behind my back! You and I have an awful lot in common."

Argan glared at Sara, who now watched Grate with distress. Grate looked at his father, with heavy, sad eyes. Steddy stared back at his son with love and composure.

"How do you have *two* sons and forsake them both?!" Hampton swung the gun around and gripped it with two hands as he pointed it at Steddy.

"She's mine!" blurted Grate.

"What?" Hampton replied.

"The baby… she's mine." He stood tall. "I'm her father."

"Is this some sort of a joke?" Hampton frowned. His eyes examined the baby, then darted across Sara, then focused on Steddy, then scanned the baby, and then studied Grate. Lastly, he glanced at Argan to make sure that she wasn't planning anything. He ran his tongue along his bottom teeth and swallowed hard. His mouth longed for more bourbon. With the gun still aimed at Steddy, Hampton turned to view the baby once again. He then peered at Grate long and hard.

"No…" he whimpered. "Were you aware of this, Steddy?" His voice was woven with pain.

"He didn't know. No one did," Grate said emphatically.

Hampton looked feverish. He slowly lowered his arm and took a couple of steps toward Grate. "But how?" He asked. He staggered a bit as lewd images flashed through his mind. "You good for nothing whore!" He barked at Sara. "I should have chosen Garla!" He pointed the gun toward her chest. "Give me the baby."

"Stop! It's not what you think. We were never…" Grate paused and glanced at Sara. "…physical."

Argan and Steddy both listened in amazement.

"Do you think that I'm stupid, cave monkey?!" Hampton aimed at Grate now.

Grate raised his hands, showing his palms, in surrender and stepped closer to Hampton. Argan discreetly inched closer to the flight deck… and Steddy.

"Your wife came to my Grandmother for help. Because you wanted a son. She wanted to make you happy. So, she drank the wild strongwater of the valley."

"What does this have to do with you?" questioned Hampton.

"I drank the water with her. And… after that moment, we became connected through our dreams."

"Your dreams?" Hampton laughed. "You must take me for an idiot!"

Argan eased closer to Steddy.

"Look, I understand how bizarre it sounds. But we only met once. And I never touched her."

"You want me to believe that this is some sort of…" he groaned and waved the gun in the air. "…some sort of *dream* baby?!" He yelled. "Preposterous!"

Grate nodded his head slowly, ashamed. Hampton wet his lips then turned to his wife and gently peeled the tape from her mouth.

"Is this true?"

"I never meant for any of this to happen," she barely voiced.

Hampton reached for the baby. Grate stepped even closer. "No, please!" cried Sara.

"Why would I ever hurt an innocent child?" Hampton asked as he took hold of the baby and began to bounce her. "She's done nothing wrong."

Sara managed an awkward smile of acceptance and relief.

Argan used her limited wave power to loosen the rope around Steddy's wrists and feet. With the hand that held the gun, Hampton moved Sara's shiny red hair from in front of her face and caressed her wet cheek. He then leaned in and passionately kissed her as the baby squirmed in between them. Grate dropped his head and looked away. Steddy was nearly freed from the ropes. Hampton opened his eyes briefly to ensure that she was enjoying the moment, but instead discovered that she was looking at Grate.

"What's this?!" he turned to Grate, then back to Sara. "Do you *love* him?" Without any delay, Hampton pointed the gun at Sara's head.

Grate sprang in her direction, in an attempt to push her out of the way, but the trigger had already been pulled. Sara fell back onto the floor, with smoke rising from the dime-sized hole in her forehead. Hampton faltered, staring down at her in shock. Grate dropped to the floor and crawled to her. Argan quickly pulled at the ropes that had Steddy bound as he wiggled free.

"You're okay. It's okay. I'm right here. I've got you," Grate whispered. He brought her arms over her body, then placed her head on his lap. Next, he moved her hair away from her beautiful face.

Hampton was appalled at the sight of the king mourning the death of *his* wife. He looked down at the healthy baby that the two had somehow created and frowned. Argan observed this and her eyes began to glow red.

"King Grate!" she shouted as she leapt toward him and covered his body with her own.

Grate felt Argan's body jolt as she sank onto him. Smoke rose from the barrel of the laser gun once more. Hampton's wicked grin of satisfaction rested in the background. Grate struggled to sit upright then saw that the laser had penetrated the left side of Argan's back… and struck her heart. Grate shuddered and looked at his father in disbelief.

Just then, Ker and the released bodyguards, James and Ben, rushed into the cabin.

"Don't shoot! He has the baby! Don't shoot!" Steddy shouted, with his hands waving in the air.

Outnumbered, Hampton pointed the laser gun at them and quickly backed out of the flight deck through a side door. Once the door closed, Ben and James raced to it, but found that it had been locked. They shot at the handle several times and were still unable to open it.

"Stay here!" James told Ben, who was the obligatory donor patient of Dr. Parlimont's eye transplant surgery.

James and Ker exited the same way that they entered in pursuit of Hampton.

"Oh, no!" Ben lamented once he turned around and realized that Sara was dead. He was still groggy from the procedure and took a seat in one of the pilot chairs.

Steddy was kneeling next to Grate, with his arm around his shoulder. Grate, now holding the limp bodies of both Sara and Argan, stared forward… stuck in a trance.

The trauma of seeing the two shot and killed caused him to forget about the Living Pools that had joined them. "Wait!" he gasped. He quickly pulled his satchel from underneath Sara and grabbed the jar. He poured it onto Argan's back, then brought the jar over Sara's head; but, the water refused her and rushed away.

"No! Please!" He reached to grab it, but the water was too fast. "Please!" He begged.

"What is this?!" Steddy asked.

Argan's cloudy eyes flew open and returned to their bright, emerald hue. She wheezed in a lungful of air then began to cough.

"Careful now… take your time." Steddy said to her as he helped her sit up and calm down, because coming back from the dead is infinitely harrowing, as one might imagine.

After several moments, Argan's gasps settled into the normal rhythm of breathing. She looked around the room and remembered where she was and why she was there. "I was with Trepor… and my parents," she said as she fell into Steddy's open arms. "What happened here?" she asked once she realized that Sara was still dead. "Did the essence not go to her? What happened?"

"Shhhh. It's alright. Don't worry about a thing. Just relax," Steddy whispered.

Argan turned to Grate, who was rocking Sara's lifeless body in his arms. Hot tears streamed down his face and rained upon her. He looked upward, praying for a miracle. Praying that the Living Pools would come back. Praying that somehow perhaps his own tears might be enough to summon her spirit and set his heart free.

Argan's throat tightened. Seeing him with her was all she needed to finally let go. She'd dedicated her entire life to the king... much more than he'd ever asked. And now she realized then that he wasn't to blame. She rose to her feet as Steddy joined her.

Ben jumped up from the chair and pointed his gun at her. Argan hissed and turned to leave.

"Stop that! Put your gun down, Benjamin," Steddy ordered. "Son?" he said to Grate. "She's leaving."

When she reached the door, Argan looked back toward the king again, but he paid her no mind. She actually laughed at herself for thinking that he would. She'd spent the last twenty or so years vying for his love. She'd defended him as if he were the Core itself. He came second to only Mother Infinity. She'd *died* for him. But now, she was tired.

"Son! Your friend is gone."

Grate gently laid Sara on the floor and kissed her lips. With fury in his eyes, he looked at his father then turned to Ben. "Give me your gun."

Delirious, Hampton ran from the spaceship and returned to his father's bedroom. He could hear his heartbeat thudding in his chest and couldn't believe that he'd shot Serenity. He ran over to his father's desk and radioed to the remaining army that backup was needed. He turned around to view his father and he froze in shock.

Dr. Parlimont was gone!

The wheelchair was also missing. Hampton searched the room with his eyes and swallowed hard to force the spicy vomit back down his throat. His head went from side to side, like a clock's pendulum, as he scanned the small room again and again. He tossed the baby and laser gun on the bed and looked underneath. Grate's weapons were still there, but nothing and no one else. Hampton then scooted back and rose to find a pistol pressing against the back of his skull.

"Raise your hands," commanded the voice.

Hampton did as he was told and slowly turned to face Grate.

"Puh- Please... please," he stammered. "Have mercy on me. We're both victims. We have both been wronged. I... I have money! You can have it all!" His teeth chattered uncontrollably.

"POW!" yelled Grate as he squeezed the gun.

Hampton squealed and fell to the ground. Unharmed.

Grate looked at the weapon in confusion. He cocked his head to the side as he inspected it in his hand.

Hampton, who'd balled up with his knees at his chest, opened his eyes and waited for pain... and Hell. But once he realized that Grate didn't know how to operate the gun, he smiled. He suddenly sprang forward to grab Grate by the knees and tackle him to the floor. This caused the gun to fly out of his hands and land across the room.

"Get off of me!" Grate shouted.

"Jungle trash!" Hampton spat as he punched him in the face until his knuckles bled. He was quite impressed with himself. His sweaty bangs clung to his forehead as he struck Grate with one final blow. He quickly surveyed the room and reached for the tubes that hung from his father's IV drip. "You should have stayed hidden away in the caves!" He grunted and wrapped the tubes around Grate's neck. "You should know which battles are worth a fight! She was mine! Do you hear me? Mine!" Sweat fell from his face.

Grate swung at Hampton and tried his best to flip him over. He gasped for air as Hampton yanked the tubes tighter and pushed down on his throat. Hampton pressed so hard that his entire body quivered. His face turned red as he watched Grate's face turn blue. A single tear rolled down the side of the king's face and branched into the edges of his hair. At last, he struggled no more. His eyes lost their light.

In that moment, the earth quaked, causing the building to tremble. An exhausted Hampton fell over to the side and stared at the ceiling as dust fell from it. Now he'd killed *two* people. He caught his breath and wallowed in the sinful satisfaction of such power. One could imagine his surprise when the door was kicked open and there stood King Grate! With Ben's gun in hand, his aim was set on Hampton, prior to him looking down.

Hampton jerked with fear and whipped his neck to view the body next to him and found his young maid, Lucille. Sheer terror emerged from the pit of his belly as he scurried backward with his rump sliding across the floor until he was stopped by the wall.

"Lucille Two," Grate uttered. Scalding pain erupted from his belly and into his chest.

Suddenly, the baby began to cry. Both men looked at her, then looked at each other. Hampton remembered the gun that flung from Lucille Two's hand and searched for it with his eyes. Just then, dark waves of Living Pools rushed into the room. They rolled over Lucille Two and crashed against the walls. Within a flash, the waves swooped in and took the gun before Hampton could reach it. He lost his balance as the tides pulled back. Grate stepped high, in pursuit of the baby girl while Hampton quickly rose and made his way to the side door that led outside. Grate shot at him twice but missed. With the baby in his arms, he waded through the knee-high water and tried to open the door that Hampton had just exited; however, the pools wouldn't allow it. He then pushed through the water toward the hallway. Steddy and Ben were wading through the halls, in search of him.

"Grate!" Steddy shouted as he met him halfway. "I wasn't going to leave without you!"

"More of Parlimont's men will be coming soon! Let's go!" Ben urged. Sirens wailed from the soldiers' barracks nearby.

They left the building through the hallway's backdoor and traipsed around to the front. Black rain was falling from the sky and it wasn't generated by the Robot's sphere.

"What sort of rain is this?!" Steddy held out his hand to catch the rainfall and watched it flee from his palms to join the flood.

"The Living Pools are fed up," Grate answered.

The water continued to rise, so the men had to use their arms as oars to help them maneuver through it. Although he tried to disguise the difficulty that he was having, Steddy's age was evident. By the time they reached the coral reef in front of the laboratory, he was depleted and unable to go any further.

Surge war horns sounded off from a distance. Grate released a sigh of relief as he knew that his warriors were close by.

"King Grate!" Ker happily shouted. His long, powerful body moved in waves atop the water. He came from around the other side of the building with James riding his back.

James was injured and holding his shoulder with his hand. "We lost Parlimont," he said.

"I am so glad to see you, Your Majesty! And you found the baby!" said Ker. He turned to his new head and smiled. "This is my spawn," he proudly announced. "It was not easy, but when I needed the help, I found the strength! And I did it!"

"It is a pleasure to serve you," the second head said with reverence.

Grate respectfully bowed his head.

"Hey, can we save the meet and greets for another time?!" James interrupted. "Doctor Parlimont and some of his men got away. They shot me in the arm. The stars only know when he'll be back to finish us." He moved his hand to reveal the wound.

Ker and the other head nodded in concord.

"So, the Robot wasn't in a coma after all… Let's return to the caves!" Grate exclaimed. "Climb onto Ker's back," he suggested to his father.

"Pardon me, I must warn you that there may or may not be pain involved. My spawn has yet to gain control of her voltage. But if he does not mind—"

"Son, look!" Steddy pointed.

Argan led the way as more than fifty Surge soldiers, on sea swallow-back swiftly coasted above the water toward the lab. Argan pushed her animal to travel faster upon seeing the men. It warmed her core to find that Grate was safe. She saw the baby in his arms and smiled.

"My King," she said once she reached him.

Grate helped his father mount behind her onto the sea swallow. James quickly transferred from Ker to join them.

"Ya'll got any of that healing water Ker told me about?" asked James.

"There's plenty where we're going. Just hold on," Grate answered before turning to Argan. "Thank you. Thank you. I don't deserve you." Tears gathered in his eyes as he stared at her.

"Where is Lucille Two?" Argan's tone begged for a favorable response and tugged at the question as she asked it.

"Yes, where is she?" echoed Ker.

The second eel head looked around and wondered who they were talking about. Grate dropped his gaze and placed his hand on Argan's knee.

"I see," she voiced. She took a deep breath, then spoke with more strength. "The entire planet is flooding. We must move quickly!"

One of the other Surges volunteered his sea swallow for Ben and Grate to ride.

"Is this thing safe?" Ben asked as his shaky hands clasped around the king's waist.

"It's much safer than here," Grate gave. "Yah! To the caves!"

A fleet of Dr. Parlimont's men approached the Surge army by motorized boats and began to shoot cannons in their direction. Since Surges were aquatic creatures, they had the advantage and quickly swam underwater to meet the opposition. With fantastic force, they punched holes into the bottom of the guard's vehicles, which caused them to fill with water and sink. Gunfire roared and smoke filled the air as the Surges grabbed the men and pulled them underwater. During battle, no individual figure could be deciphered. Only their splashing could be seen, and cries of battle could be heard.

Chapter Twenty-Four: The Faithful Dance of Mother Infinity

Grate held the baby close to him as they raced through The Stretch at top speeds. They were almost to the caves. Grate's heart was beating so hard that he wondered if it would give out on him. He looked down at his daughter and felt a tender courage in places that he didn't know existed. All he wanted to do was to see her thrive.

Just then, a bang was heard behind them and a something whizzed by Grate's head. Then another. And another.

"Everyone, DOWN!" he yelled. He covered the baby with his body and glanced behind him.

Dr. Parlimont and five of his men were gaining up them in a sleek motorized boat that had both large treaded tires and a propeller. They were shooting bullets and spears at them.

"Careful, you fools! They have my granddaughter!" spat Parlimont. He grabbed a voice amplifier from beside his seat and called out to them. "Give me the child or else! I will not stop until I have her!"

"Arrghh!" Ker hollered once he was hit with a series of bullets.

"Faster! We've got to lose them!" Grate urged.

Suddenly the sea swallow that Argan, Steddy, and James were riding abruptly twitched and began to slow down. Next, it appeared to swim backwards, despite Argan's commands.

"Oh, no! Come on, come on," pleaded Argan before realizing that her animal had been harpooned and was being reeled in by Parlimont's boat. "King!" she called out.

Grate's stomach burned with despair. He knew that he had to go back for Argan and his father, but he also didn't want to put his daughter in harm's way. He turned to the side and watched Ben from his peripheral vision. "Here, take her! Protect her."

Ben nodded and secured the baby between his legs and hovered over her as Grate turned his animal around and dashed to save the others. Steddy, James, and Argan had thrown themselves into the water and continued to swim forward. Argan wrapped

James's arms around her neck to carry him on her back and pulled Steddy by the shirt collar through the water. Ker slithered above the water and propelled his body in their direction to create a wave that would boost them forward.

"Butler!" Dr. Parlimont's voice cracked through the amplifier, "Where is that baby?!" After realizing that none of the swimmers were holding the infant, Parlimont ordered for the guards to "shoot him." Perhaps it was the sounds of the crashing waves, the sight of the two-headed eel, or the stings from the black rainfall, but they misunderstood and fired at Grate.

"Oomf!" Grate moaned as he fell back onto Ben and off the sea swallow.

A small harpoon had struck him through the right shoulder.

He inadvertently pulled Ben into the water with him and struggled to stay alert. Argan released a high-pitched whistle and swam even faster toward him.

"Move your legs! Help me, before I let the two of you drown!" she shouted to Steddy and James as she rushed to help with the baby.

"King! Nooooo!" Ker bellowed. "NO MORE!"

A white wall of water rose along the side of the eel as he whirled around and advanced toward Dr. Parlimont's boat as fast as possible. "Give your all, sweet daughter! Until the end!" he told his spawn as their tails vibrated and radiated like never before. The eel's flesh absorbed each bullet and harpoon that was shot its way. The two heads leaned forward right before crashing into Parlimont's boat and created a tremendous explosion on impact. The black water suddenly became pellucid and even choppier than before. It tossed everyone about like pieces of dust in the wind. James, Argan, and Steddy were torn from each other and the baby flew from Ben's arms as they were sucked into an underwater current. Ben swam toward the infant with all of his might and pushed as hard as his body would go, but it was of no use. He stayed underwater until his lungs began to burn and knew that he had to return to the surface... for what good would he be if he drowned?

The baby girl's pink blanket unwrapped from around her and drifted away as she peacefully floated through the water. She kicked her little feet and gnawed at her tiny fist with her gums. Grate opened his eyes and saw his precious baby pass by. He was almost certain that there were three gill-like slits along her sides. He rubbed his eyes in disbelief and swam toward her. Just then, a gray woman, who had a long fin instead of legs and long, dark green hair, rose from underneath him. She stared at the handsome king and blocked his view of the baby. He reached for the infant and tried to swim around the mermaid; however, the fish-tailed woman was much stronger than she appeared and merely held him down by the shoulder. She giggled and then bit the line that was connected to the spear in his shoulder. Next, she snapped the metal rod with little effort and removed both halves from his flesh. Hundreds of gigantic bubbles escaped his mouth as Grate screamed underwater. She then took him by the wrist to pull him above the water. He choked for a while as his lungs punished him for the wait. Argan, Steddy, James, and Ben were also safe, and accompanied by a mermaid each. The flooding was now above everyone's chins.

"Where's my baby?!" Grate demanded from the group. His eyes quickly scanned the arms of everyone there as he treaded the water. He found it interesting that despite all the dangers he'd encountered through life, the thought of losing an infant that he'd just met was the most horrifying of all. But he knew. He knew her the moment he saw her. He knew the light that rested inside of her eyes. And the familiar smile that never left the corners of her mouth.

"It's alright, son," said Steddy with a calming assurance. "She's right here. Eating," he smiled and looked at the mermaid, whose back he was holding.

Ignoring the intense pain in his arm, Grate pushed forward and reached his father within several strokes. The others drew closer to join them.

"Where is she?"

"Down here," Steddy whispered as he pointed to the mermaid.

The gray creature then rose just enough for her midsection to show above water. She touched her lower belly with her large, webbed hand and pulled open a fleshy pouch that revealed the baby nursing inside. The newborn rested, in a scarce amount of water, curled up against the mermaid. Her gills slowly opened and closed as she nursed. Ben wiped his remaining eye in amazement.

"Hey, James, you're seeing this, too right?"

"Man, I'm seeing… I'm seeing," he responded with large eyes.

"Your daughter was hungry," Argan said with surprise.

Grate smiled and turned to the mermaid. "Thank you so very much, madam."

The nursing mermaid bowed her head in response.

"They were kind enough to offer to take us to the caves. The water will be over our heads soon," Argan mentioned. The gills along the side of her face slowly opened and closed.

"Thank the stars the caves are upland. Come on, everybody. Let's go!" ordered Grate.

Everyone got behind a mermaid and secured himself by locking each arm underneath the mermaid's arms. Argan looked back at the wreckage. An aroma of charred metal, plastic, and flesh sailed through the air. Parlimont's boat was scattered across the water in countless pieces. Human bodies were bobbing face down in the water, but there was no eel. She realized that this was the faithful dance of Mother Infinity. There was a loss with every gain. It had to be that way.

Chapter Twenty-Five: The Onyx Caves

The Onyx Caves were busy with panic and arguing. Elder Surges, who were known for their extreme water-persuading powers, stood at cave entrances with their arms held above their heads, and kept the flooding waters at bay. The Living Pools were many things, but disrespectful wasn't one of them. The few remaining adult Surges rallied the young together and prepared for battle since their leaders hadn't returned.

Lucille sat on her grandmother's bed, with her brothers in her arms. She observed the old woman's blissful expression and envied her. None of the Surges would tell her what was going on outside and she had a sickening feeling that they wouldn't be able to find sanctuary within the cave walls for long. She felt alone and unwanted. She couldn't go home and the caves would never be her home.

"At least I have the two of you," she reasoned as placed helmets that she'd carved from turtle shells, on her brothers' heads. Then she tied the wrap-carrier around her neck and placed the boys inside. *Flash*. A familiar figure rushed by the cabin entrance.

"Hey! Stop!" Lucille yelled while shuffling off the bed. "Pankto!"

After a couple of seconds, a teenage Surge peeked inside of the king's chamber.

"I knew it was you!" Lucille tiptoed to the doorway and blushed a bit. She and Pankto had become close after he'd given her some pink strongwater to drink to stop her nightmares.

"Hello, Lucille." Pankto nervously looked from side to side. "I cannot stay."

"What's going on? Please tell me."

"I do not know."

"You know *something*... more than I do. I'm so afraid, Pankto. And alone. I'm scared that everyone's forgotten about us."

He rested his hand on Lucille's shoulder. "Stay here with your Grandmother. We will do everything in our power to make sure that you and your family stay safe."

"Are we in danger? Where is Cousin Grate?"

"The King has not returned. I have been called to prepare for battle."

"But your powers and gifts haven't been confirmed yet."

"Do not worry. Although I am premature, I am strong for my age. I have finally disclosed that my power is the ability to hear the thoughts of others," he leaned in and whispered. "I may also have the ancestral gift of an electric tail."

Lucille wasn't listening to him. She thought of her mother and considered sneaking out and returning home.

"Lucille, do not be a fool. If you leave the caves, you will die."

Her cheeks turned red from embarrassment.

"Remain calm," Pankto gently said before motioning toward the Godmother. "She has enjoyed your company and likes when you sing to her. I must go now."

"Huh? How do you know that? Pankto!"

But he was gone. Lucille scratched her neck and nibbled at her bottom lip. She'd never felt so small. Growing up, she'd been proud to belong to the family of Steddy Waters, the Godmother, and even the refugee king. But when she walked into the Parlimont mansion and learned the lifestyle of the wealthy, she felt silly for feeling important. She'd felt special for having her mother's map but was once again reminded of how big the world was when she became stranded in the wilderness. Then, upon arriving in the caves, any sense of happiness or self-worth was fleeting, as she felt more insignificant than ever with all the Surges rush past her and act as if she was just a piece of furniture. She took a deep breath and poked her head outside of the chamber.

The mermaids stopped in front of the caves, as that's where the waters stopped. Steddy and the guards stared in amazement at the Surges, who were warding off the water. The mermaid that had been nursing the baby gently cradled her in her arms and gave her a loving hug before passing her to Grate. Argan thanked the mermaids and urged Steddy, Ben, and James to keep up. Surges greeted them with berries, wine, and jars of healing water and cheered.

"King Grate is here!"

"He is alive!"

"Oh, thank the stars and Eternity All Mighty!"

"We knew you would find him, Argan!"

Steddy, James, and Ben were skeptical at first when the Surges approached them with the healing water but became grateful beyond belief once their injuries were reversed and their wounds were closed.

"Hey, excuse me... can you do something about my missing eye?" asked Ben.

"No. The healing water only heals. It does not grow new body parts," answered a Surge.

Ben cursed under his breath.

"The elders will not be able to control the floods forever," Argan whispered to Grate as they entered the cave. "We must think of a plan... quickly!"

"You're right." He spoke in a guttural voice as one of the Surges poured the pink strongwater onto his wounded shoulder. He winked at Argan then kissed the top of the baby's small head.

A group of young Surges ran through the caves and didn't notice Lucille standing in the shadows with her back against the wall. After their echoes could no longer be heard, she dashed in another direction, where sunlight could be seen. She approached an opening that was several feet in the air and big enough for them to fit through. There was no way to determine when Surges would arrive to that section of the cave, so she moved quickly. By using the grooves and humps of the wall, Lucille was able to climb up to the opening without trouble and crawl through.

"Does the infant need milk?" A one-armed Surge asked Argan.

"Not at this time."

"How's my Grandmother?" Grate marched to his chamber.

"Your Grandmother is well, although still asleep. Your cousins are with her," the Surge reported as she followed the group.

"Cousins... right," Grate moaned.

"Cousins?" asked Steddy, who followed behind with James and Ben.

"A little girl told me that Lucille and the boys are here," James whispered to him.

"What?! How?" Steddy asked.

"Who knows." James shrugged, "And check this, the girl looked *just* like Lucille. I mean exactly like her. Pigtails and all!"

Ben nodded. "It's true. The girl untied us. She saved us!"

"Where is Margot?" Steddy inquired.

Ben and James looked at one another. "We don't know."

"There are Elders at every exit, Your Majesty," continued the one-armed Surge. "And the adolescents are being armed and arranged for battle as we speak. The high opening on the east side is the only exit not patrolled."

The king sped up as he approached his bedroom and nearly ran the moment he saw his Grandmother. Steddy stopped at the door.

"I have her, Momma!" He kissed his Grandmother's hand. "Look at her. Isn't she beautiful? She's perfect." Grate kneeled beside the bed and placed the baby on a pillow, next to the old woman.

The men stared in awe at the sight of the defenseless matriarch.

"What's wrong with her?" Steddy asked Argan. He finally got the strength to move his heavy feet and walk into the room.

"No one knows. She has been trapped by this deep slumber for days." Argan looked around the room and frowned. "Where are the others? Where are the young?"

Lucille tumbled down the outside of the cave and landed on the ground with a splash. Fat droplets of rain rapped on her head. She held out her hands and stared at the sky. She'd never seen rain before. She found herself sitting in about three feet of water and wondered if that was the reason for the Surges' concern. Just as she was about to taste the water that had collected in her palm, Lucille heard whimpers and sniffling around the corner. She felt compelled to find whoever it was and offer support. She stood and quietly approached the source of the crying. She knew all too well the misery of feeling small, helpless, worthless, and alone. She desperately wanted to meet the person, who shared her level of grief and sadness.

"Find the girl!" Argan shouted to the one-armed Surge.

"Find the human girl!" yelled the Surge as she ran out of the chamber and throughout other parts of the caves.

"I will help them," Argan said to Grate before leaving.

Grate nodded and touched his Grandmother's hand.

"Could ya'll give us a second, guys?" Steddy asked the bodyguards while looking down at his wet loafers. He stepped forward and approached Grate.

James and Ben walked to the entrance of the bedroom chamber and kept their backs turned.

"Man, I still can't believe Doctor Parlimont took my eye!" whispered Ben. "They were the best thing about me! When's the last time you saw a brother with light blue eyes?!"

"Son, a word?" Steddy said as he approached the Godmother's bed.

Grate rose and faced his father. His father looked up to him now. He remembered when his father was a mountain to him.

"I don't know where to start, but I want to say I'm sorry."

"Don't," replied Grate. "We don't need to do this."

"But I want to. I need you to know how I feel."

"I don't need to know anything!" Grate threw up his hands then turned away and walked in a small circle. "I'm a man now. It's too late for all that!"

"No, son. It's not too late. Listen…I know you think I left you—"

"Which you did."

"…And went to raise Hampton Junior—"

"Which you did!" Grate shook his head and looked back at his daughter.

"Son, no. Look at me. Listen to me, please. You fell into a coma when we first got here. You were dying. I was out of money and the doctors had given up on you. So, I went to see Ol' Parlimont and ended up trading my freedom for a remedy."

"What? Momma never told me any of this."

"Well. She wouldn't have anything to do with me after that. It broke her heart that I went to see Parlimont after what he did to your Mother."

Grate swallowed hard.

"He threatened to isolate you until you improved. And I know what that meant coming from him! You were only five years old," his voice shook. "You were all I had left, son. I was desperate." Steddy held back tears.

"Didn't you wonder about me? Wonder how I looked or how big I'd gotten?"

"Son, of course!"

"Didn't you miss me?"

"Everyday—"

"I was angry for so long. For *so* long! I hated you!" Grate's bottom lip trembled as a single tear ran down his face. "I thought you'd chosen them over me."

"No! I would never- I want to be in your life, Grate. Stay in your life. And in my grandbaby's life. If you'll let me..." Steddy held out his arms and waited.

Grate stepped closer to his father and embraced him.

"I'm so sorry. I love you." Steddy patted his son's back.

"I love you too, Dad."

"Steddy?" gave an old woman's scratchy voice. "Is that you?"

Chapter Twenty-Six: Home

Lucille stretched her neck to view around the hill and hopefully find whoever was crying. She uncontrollably gasped in horror and quickly placed her hand over her mouth while she backed away. It was Mr. Parlimont!

She clenched her teeth and hunched her shoulders as she tried to stealthily race back to the hole in the cave without making any splashing sounds. Regardless of whether it was the gasp or the footsteps, he'd heard Lucille. He crawled to the side of the hill to see who he'd heard then abruptly rose to his feet while still moving forward so that he could catch up with the girl.

"Lucille!" he cried.

The curious water turned from black, to green, to yellow as it rushed toward Lucille and crashed against the cave wall while she climbed.

"Ahhh! Help me! Someone, please!" she screamed.

"Lucille! No, wait!" He awkwardly jogged through the water with his knees coming up to his chest.

Lucille climbed the rock and scraped the fronts of her legs in the process. The rain began to fall harder as the water crept up the wall to follow her. Lucille couldn't believe that she had run into him *and* was showing Parlimont the way to the Surges' home. Hastily, she crawled on her hands and knees through the opening that led to the Onyx caves. She thought of her Grandmother's bed in the king's chamber and wished she were there instead. Finally, without hesitation, she turned to her side and slid down the bumpy wall to the floor. Yellow water poured in behind her.

"Do ya'll hear screaming?" asked the Godmother. She was sitting up and holding a cup of tea that a Surge has just brought to her.

"The warriors will handle it," Grate answered. "I'm just glad you're alright! I was so worried. Are you sure you're alright?"

"It's good to see you, Mom. I'm glad you're back. Here, let me help you with that." Steddy stood next to the bed and reached for the hot tea.

"No, I'm fine," she insisted. She looked her son up and down for a moment. "It's good to see you too, Sted. I'm glad *you're* back," she grinned before taking a sip. "Grate, catch me up on what's going on around here."

All at once, a frothy tide of yellow water flooded into the chamber from the right. A wide-eyed Lucille came sloshing in shortly after.

"Mister- Mister Parlimont is here! In the caves!" she panted.

James, Ben, Steddy, and Grate ran toward her.
"Get inside!" Steddy urged.

The one-armed Surge from before returned and bowed before the King. "The caves are flooding! You cannot stay here, King! We must get your family to safety!"

"There's an intruder here! Protect my family and pack for a year's journey!" Grate grabbed a new set of weapons from a corner of his room then slid past the group in search of Parlimont.

It didn't take long for him to find him. Hampton looked horrible.

"Stop right there! Put your hands up!" Grate shouted.
"King Grate, it is me!"
Grate squinted his eyes as Hampton, with his hands raised, transformed into Garla, Argan, and lastly, Lucille.
"Haha! Lucille Two!" Grate exclaimed. He picked her up in the air and swung her around before hugging her tightly.
"I cannot breathe, King Grate!"
Oh, I'm sorry. I'm just," the king wet his lips and paused to catch he breath. "I'm so happy to see you!"
"I am happy to see you, too."
"Why would you ever take on *his* form? You almost got yourself killed!"
"Again."
"Ooh. Right. Again. Did the Living Pools bring you back?"
Lucille Two nodded. Grate thought of Sara.
Lucille Two sighed and looked down at the water that was now above her waist. "The Pools no longer agree to share the land."
"I see. And I don't blame them. Come, let's go meet the others."
Lucille Two shifted into a bright, orange fire fairy and followed the king through the caves.

They joined everyone at the main entrance of the Onyx Caves. As Grate had requested, the Surges were in a hurry packing enough food, water, clothing, and other supplies to last them a year. Surges held both sides of gigantic crater leaves over the humans, so they'd stay dry in the rainfall. The Godmother was waiting on the king's sea swallow and holding the baby in a soft, tan blanket. Argan, Lucille, and her brothers were waiting on another animal while Steddy, Ben, and James mounted on a sea swallow that the one-armed Surge was to drive.

With the fire fairy by his side and a voice-amplifying coral horn hanging from his neck, Grate mounted his animal then raised his eyebrows at Argan. She couldn't contain her smile.

"It is good to see you, Lucille Two," she exclaimed.

Lucille Two floated to Argan and kissed her on the nose before resting on her shoulder.

"I see you didn't forget your walking stick, Momma. How you feeling?" asked Grate while admiring his daughter.

"I'm just fine. What's the plan, son?"

"Home."

Chapter Twenty-Seven: The Omega Light

Grate, his family, the army of Surges, and a pod of mermaids dashed through the rain, past The Stretch and into The Community. By this time the water was a lovely, clear turquoise color and deeper than five feet. Community members were sitting on their roofs, with nowhere to go.

"Come with us to dry land! Come with us and be saved!" Grate shouted as Surges and mermaids helped the stranded people onto sea swallows. Many of them thanked the king profusely for his unselfishness. And then there were others, who surprisingly, chose to stay in the rain and refused to be helped by "monsters."

The group continued their quest as they made their way to The Pasturage. Most of the families, in their multi-level homes, were not alarmed… or at least didn't appear to be. Members of The

Pasturage laughed at and mocked the king and his bunch. Only a few wealthy families, and several homeworkers joined them.

"Wait, we can't leave! I don't see my mother! Uncle Steddy, tell Cousin Grate to look again," Lucille begged.

Members of The Community looked away in shame and pity.

They rode through the streets of the shopping area, hospital, and golf course in search of anyone who wanted to come along. King Grate yelled through the coral horn until his voice became raspy and his throat became sore.

Buzzing sounds could be heard from afar.

"Look!" giggled a chubby, little boy as he pointed to the sky and held on to his mother, who held on to a mermaid.

A vast sheet of colorful, twinkling lights flew above them and caused the falling rain to evaporate. The fire fairies had left the forest to check on the king since this was the first time they'd witnessed the Living Pools behaving in such a manner.

"Would you take a look at that!" gasped the Godmother as she revered the dazzling fairy entourage above.

The rain began to fall harder outside of the fire fairy canopy. Grate reached into his satchel and retrieved the map of the planet then looked ahead.

"It won't be much longer! We're almost there!" he announced through the horn.

Suddenly, a thunderous noise was heard overhead. Everyone cowered in fear as massive cracks appeared across the sphere's surface. People began to cry and scream. Others demanded an explanation for what was happening with the planet. A small group cursed at Grate for bringing them along and demanded to be taken back to their homes. The fire fairies began to flash their lights brighter and quicker than before.

"Can't this thing go any faster?" asked the Godmother.

"Let's find out. Yah! Yah!!" said the king. "Forward, everybody! Come on!"

In the distance, only the spaceship could be seen, since the water had risen above the laboratory. Argan eyed the king as she tried to figure out what he had in mind.

"Help! Help me!" cried a voice.

"Did you hear that?" Grate asked his Grandmother. He looked amongst the floating debris then turned to his soldiers. "Someone's out there!" he shouted.

"Help me, please! Please!!" the voice coughed.

After a while, a figure could be seen holding onto the top of the coral reef mound that sat in front of the lab.

"It's Mister Parlimont!" someone announced.
"The bastard!" spat the Godmother.

Grate slowed his sea swallow and steered in the direction of mound. The flashing lights on Hampton's necklace shown through the rain. Argan growled. Grate lifted the horn to his lips.
"Remove the neck piece and put your hands up!" he ordered.
"Grate, don't!" urged Steddy. "Everybody doesn't deserve a second chance."
"He tried to *kill* you!" added the Godmother.
"We're the same, Pop." Grate looked back at the Godmother, who was shaking her head and holding the baby close, then signaled for a Surge to rescue the Parlimont heir. "I owe it to him, Momma." He faced forward and watched Hampton struggle to stay afloat in the

"Hey! Make sure he doesn't have any weapons!" commanded the king.

Everyone silently watched as Hampton removed the ring from around his neck and humbly climbed onto the sea swallow. Grate rode past and advanced to the space shuttle.
"Th-- thank you," uttered a shivering Parlimont.

The bottom compartment of the ship was still open; but due to its size, the water hadn't reached the inside. Cracks continued to appear and spread across the glass of the sphere.

"Everyone, board carefully!" ordered the king while he assisted his Grandmother with the baby. He glanced at Hampton, who watched him from a distance.

Argan approached Hampton and shoved him in the chest. "You will wait until everyone else is on," she hissed. She fixed her ruby eyes on him and refused to look away.

Some of the Surges and mermaids helped people up the ramp while others packed the shuttle with the goods brought from the caves. Once the Godmother and baby were secured in a suite, the king found Steddy, Ben, and James near the cockpit.

"Hey, James. I remember you mentioning that you worked for the Space Center back in the day," said Grate.

"Yeah…" James nervously replied.

"What's going on in that noggin, Grate? There's no place to go," Steddy interrupted.

"Look over here," Grate bit his bottom lip as he jogged backwards to a telescope that faced out into Mother Infinity. He grabbed a sketch from his pocket that he'd taken from the lab and quickly repositioned the machine. "Take a look," he said with a heavy sigh.

"Good gracious!" shouted Steddy.

"Couldn't be!" said James

"I better have a seat!" Ben rubbed his forehead and plumped himself down in a chair.

Grate looked concerned. "Can you do it, James? Can you get us there?"

James took a moment to inspect the dashboard and turn a few switches on the panel. "Yeah," he nodded. "Yeah. I believe I can. This thing's in great shape."

"King Grate, please excuse me." The one-armed Surge stopped at the entrance of the cabin.

"Yes. What is it?"

"All of the humans are inside. Your packages have been secured as well," she proudly reported.

"Thank you." Grate turned to James. "I've got to run outside, man. Are you sure we can make it home in one piece?"

"Yeah! I'm feeling good about this. It's all coming back to me, brother."

Grate then followed the Surge out onto the ramp to find the mermaids, fire faires, and Surges waiting for him. His stomach tightened once his eyes met Argan.

"I thought you said everyone was on," he said to the Surge.

"Oh. My apologies, King Grate. She held him until the end."

Grate nodded. "Hampton, do I have your word that you won't harm anyone on this ship?"

"I promise," he replied with a dramatic bow.

"Please allow him to board, Argan."

After a moment, Argan released Hampton's arm and shoved him one final time.

"I can't thank you all enough!" Grate yelled to the crowd. "I will miss you. All of you!" He looked at Argan and quickly looked away. "This will always be my home."

"Three cheers for King Grate!" yelled a portly Surge.

Grate looked at Argan once again and couldn't stop his feet from moving in her direction. He couldn't hear the cheers or feel the rain drops or see the twinkling fairies that sparkled in his honor. He only saw her.

"Argan."

"Yes, Grate?" she sniffled.

"Come with me."

"No."

"Please?"

"I cannot. Not this time."

"Then I'll miss you, for as long as I live."

"I will miss you, too. Forever."

"And I love you—"

The glass sphere began to break even more. Everyone looked upward and saw that the outer pools were seeping through the barrier. The water around them started rising faster than ever.

"Gotcha!" grunted Nicholas, who'd been lurking in the wings. He grabbed Grate from behind and wrapped his arm around his neck. He held a small diamond-shaped metal devise to the side of the king's head. "Nobody move!"

"Don't do anything you'll regret. You have a chance at a new life. A new start," Grate whispered.

Argan's eyes glowed bright red.

"Warn your little pet that I'm holding a bomb to your neck. And if she makes any false moves, I'll blow us all up into a million pieces…"

"Alright. Alright. Stay cool. What is it you want?"

"Let's see… what do I want?" Hampton slung his hair from his face and stuck out his tongue to moisten his dry bottom lip. "I want a woman, who truly loves me! I want a baby, who lives past a week! And I want a father…" His voice trailed off.

Grate thought of his daughter. "You're better than this. Please don't do this, man!"

"Well I'm doing it!" he laughed. He tightened his grip on the tiny bomb and started to squeeze the button.

Just then, a gunshot was heard, and Hampton's body jerked before going limp and falling onto the ramp.

"Pow!" whispered Lucile Two. She'd reassumed her form as the human girl.

Grate retrieved the miniature bomb from the floor and passed it to Argan. The mermaids quickly grabbed Hampton's body as he begged for mercy and slid him down the ramp to beneath the water. The ground trembled as the sphere opened even more.

"You must go, Grate! Now!" warned Argan.

He nodded then removed the gun from Lucille Two's small hands.

"You just saved us all, Lucille Two. I can never repay you. You're a hero."

"There is no need for payment. I am your friend."

"Well, are you staying or going, my friend?"

"I will go where you go, King Grate," she smiled.

"Let's go then."

Grate stared at Argan until the bottom ramp retracted and the lower compartment closed. Then, he and Lucille Two hurried to the cockpit and fastened their safety belts.

"There you are! I thought we were going to have to head back without ya," Ben joked.

"Nah, never that. Let's go!" Grate rubbed his hands together and released a long sigh of relief.

"What's Lucille doing up here?" asked Steddy.

"I am not Lucille. I am Lucille Two."

"I'll explain everything on the way," Grate chuckled. "How we looking up there?"

"It's looking good. It's all good," James responded with a nod. "Ben, count me down from ten."

"Ten… nine… eight… seven…"

The giant engines roared, and the spaceship vibrated as they prepared for takeoff.

Grate turned to his father. "Hey Pop, how do you like the name Lumé?"

"Lumé Watters… I like that," Steddy said with a nod of approval.

"My little Lumé."